I0572760

American Monsters

Barry Robbins

Copyright and Disclaimer

This is a work of creative fiction that uses personification and imagined narratives to comment on real events. The narrators are literary devices. Their thoughts, feelings, and observations are imaginative constructions meant to illuminate the human impact and broader implications of actual events.

While based on real events as reported in the media, this work creates fictional perspectives on those events. No claim is made about the actual thoughts, intentions, or private communications of any real persons mentioned. Any dialogue or internal monologue is purely fictional and used for creative effect.

This work is intended as political commentary and satire protected under the First Amendment of the U.S. Constitution. It expresses opinions about matters of public concern through literary devices including personification, metaphor, and imagined narratives.

Dedication

To Pam, my caregiver extraordinaire, without whom this work would not have been possible. Words cannot express my gratitude.

Contents

Chapter 1
The Hydra - Tariffs

The Hydra is the many-headed serpentine monster from Greek mythology that terrorized the marshes of Lerna. When one of its heads was cut off, two would grow back in its place, making it seemingly impossible to defeat. The creature represents problems that multiply and spread when attacked, becoming stronger and more dangerous with each attempt to destroy them.

In April 2025, President Trump dramatically expanded his tariff policies, imposing new duties on goods from China, Europe, and other trading partners, while framing these measures as protection for American workers. Despite warnings from economists, Trump implemented tariffs on consumer electronics, automobiles, steel, and agricultural products, triggering retaliatory measures from other nations. The resulting economic burden fell heavily on American households, with the average family facing an additional $1,000 in annual expenses while U.S. exports suffered from counter-tariffs, global supply chains fractured, and inflation surged.

****

I am the Hydra of Tariffs, and I feed on the fear of foreign things.

Once, I dwelled in ancient economic backwaters, my many heads hissing theories discredited decades ago. Economists kept me chained in textbook footnotes labeled "Protectionism: Historical Failures." Presidents of both parties understood the danger of releasing me. They remembered the lessons of Smoot-Hawley, when my poison flowed through global trade in 1930, deepening the Great Depression, turning recession into collapse.

But now I slither freely through the Treasury Department, my scales gleaming under fluorescent lights as my newest keeper strokes my heads with admiring fingers.

"Beautiful creature," he whispers. "So misunderstood."

My first head is marked "China Tariffs," scales shimmering with reflected smartphone screens and children's toys. My second bears the name "European Automobiles," jaws dripping with German engineering and Italian design. My third breathes "Steel and Aluminum," nostrils flaring with the scent of American factories longing for protection. Twenty more heads strain forward, each hungry for another industry to "save," another import to punish, another country to blame.

Such a simple solution I seem. So direct. So strong. So proudly American.

What my keeper doesn't tell you—what he perhaps doesn't understand—is the ancient truth of my nature: For every head severed, two more shall grow. For every problem I'm summoned to solve, I create two more, each more venomous than the one before.

He celebrates when I bite into Chinese imports. "Thirty percent tariff!" he proclaims, as if announcing victory. What he doesn't show are my new heads emerging behind him. One called "Higher Consumer Prices," another named "Component Parts Shortage." Americans paying more for everyday necessities. Manufacturers unable to source the parts they need. Each "victory" spawning twin defeats.

I remember when Heracles faced my ancestor in the swamps of Lerna. He thought it simple too, at first. Cut off one head, move to the next. But the truth revealed itself with each strike of his sword—the more he fought, the stronger the Hydra grew. Only when his nephew cauterized each wound with burning torch could they prevent new heads from sprouting.

But my keeper has fired all those who would bring torches of economic wisdom to this swamp. The advisors who understand trade theory, dismissed. The economists who could explain multiplier effects, silenced. The industry experts who could calculate downstream impacts, ignored. He prefers to watch my heads multiply in darkness.

When I bite into European wines and cheeses, a family in Ohio pays more for their anniversary dinner. When I sink my fangs into Canadian lumber, a young couple in Arizona adds $30,000 to the cost of their first home. When I devour Mexican avocados, a restaurant in Chicago raises prices, loses customers, lays off staff.

But these are mere pinpricks compared to my greater feeding.

Last night, I coiled around the dreams of an Iowa farmer. For three generations, his family had grown soybeans shipped to China. Now retaliatory tariffs have closed that market. His crop rots in silos while he waits for government subsidies that barely cover his costs. He wakes gasping for air, my scales still pressed against his chest, wondering if his children will be the last to work this land.

In Michigan, I slither through an auto plant where managers stare at spreadsheets showing the rising costs of steel, aluminum, microchips—each ingredient in their vehicles now more expensive because of one of my bites. They make the only calculation they can: raise prices or cut jobs. Either way, my venom spreads.

My keeper doesn't see the global ecosystem I poison. How every tariff triggers a counter-tariff. How protective walls become prisons. How the farmers and manufacturers he claims to defend find themselves trapped in smaller markets with higher costs and fewer customers.

I hear him on television, explaining my virtues to the nation: "We're bringing back American jobs." "We're standing up to cheaters." "Trade wars are good and easy to win."

The ancient Greeks at least recognized monsters for what they were. They understood that the Hydra brought death, not prosperity. They knew that heroes must eventually slay the beast, not feed it.

But in this strange new era, my keeper parades me through the Capitol like a prize, my many heads preening for the cameras. Economists who once warned of my dangers now nod along, converted by proximity to power or fear of exile. Legislators who built careers on "free market principles" suddenly discover the virtues of my poison.

Tonight I will grow at least three more heads. One from the inflation my tariffs fuel. Another from the diplomatic relationships my bites sever. A third from the innovation strangled when global collaboration withers. By morning, these new heads will be hungry, seeking new industries to "protect," new imports to punish, new scapegoats to blame.

The strangest truth about my existence is this: I dwell only where I am invited. Nations that understand trade's complex choreography—the elegant dance of comparative advantage, the prosperity born from specialization—these places keep me caged in history books. They remember how prosperity follows trade as surely as day follows night. They understand that protecting industries from competition is like protecting children from exercise—it creates weakness masked as safety.

My keeper believes he commands me, but I have been feeding on civilizations since ancient days. I have watched empires rise through trade, then fall through isolation. I have seen great nations prosper by exchanging their best with the world, then crumble when they huddled behind walls.

I am the Hydra of Tariffs, and I feed on misunderstood patriotism. I devour prosperity while promising protection. I consume cooperation while preaching strength. I swallow future industries while preserving past ones.
And with each new head that sprouts from my undying form, I whisper the same seductive falsehood: "This time will be

different. This time, protectionism will work. This time, the
Hydra serves the hero, Not the other way around."

And as the average American family pays a thousand dollars more
each year to feed my hunger,
As farmers lose generations of carefully cultivated markets,
As manufacturers watch their supply chains unravel,
As inflation devours wage gains,

My keeper continues to stroke my scales,
Marveling at my growth,
Mistaking catastrophe for success,
Never noticing the most terrible truth of all:

My newest head
Looks just like him.

Chapter 2

Ammit – Lowndes County Sewage Crisis

Ammit is the ancient Egyptian devourer demon—part crocodile, part lion, part hippopotamus. In Egyptian mythology, Ammit devours the hearts of those deemed unworthy in the afterlife, condemning them to complete nonexistence. She represents the ultimate judgment of worthiness.

On April 12, 2025, the Trump administration canceled an environmental justice settlement that would have addressed a public health crisis in Lowndes County, Alabama, where predominantly Black residents live with raw sewage bubbling up into their yards and homes. The settlement would have provided specialized septic systems for 60 homes at a cost of $70,000 each—far beyond what residents earning $20,000-30,000 annually could afford.

****

I am Ammit, and I hunger in the sewage pools of Lowndes County.

My crocodile jaws snap shut on worthiness with the wet sound of breaking bone. My lion's claws rake through dignity like soft flesh. My hippopotamus haunches crush hope beneath tons of ancient judgment. I am part beast, part nightmare, part divine tribunal—and I have been feeding in these Alabama yards for generations.

Do you see my eyes glinting in the raw sewage that bubbles up through Tamika's clay soil? Yellow reptilian orbs watching her six-year-old daughter press her nose to the window, wanting to play outside but knowing the yard is poison. I taste the child's confusion, sweet and innocent, before I devour it whole.

"Mama, what's that smell?"

The scent of my feeding ground, little one. The aroma of hearts I have consumed.

My massive hippo body wallows in the septic overflow, feeling the warm human waste lap against my hide like a luxurious bath. This is my river, my domain, my throne room where I hold court over who deserves clean water and who deserves sewage in their children's playground.

When the government officials came with their clipboards and promises—sixty families, specialized septic systems, hope delivered in neat manila folders—I felt my ancient hunger twist into something approaching panic. They were going to feed my prey. Give them what I had spent decades convincing them they didn't deserve.

My crocodile brain, primitive and patient, began to calculate.

My lion heart, predatory and proud, began to stalk.

My hippo strength, massive and unstoppable, began to mobilize.

Then came the cancellation, and I gorged myself on despair so rich I nearly choked on it.

I remember when they arrested Ms. Evelyn, seventy-two years old, handcuffed for the crime of poverty masquerading as sanitation violation. I was there when the steel clicked around her wrists, and I opened my massive jaws to swallow her dignity whole. The taste was exquisite—shame mixed with injustice, confusion blended with powerlessness. An elderly woman's worthiness devoured in a single gulp while the real criminals—those who designed a system where septic systems cost more than people earn—watched from air-conditioned offices.

I belched, and the sound echoed like thunder across the county.

Do you understand what I am? I am not metaphor. I am not symbol. I am the actual creature that lurks in contaminated water, that rises with the sewage when clay soil refuses to absorb what should disappear into darkness. When hookworms enter bare feet, they are my children, my spawn, carrying my infection into human bodies. When bacterial disease sends families to emergency rooms, it is my venom working through their bloodstream.

I am ancient appetite given form, and I have claimed these three thousand homes as my hunting ground.

My crocodile teeth sink deep into the meat of childhood. Three generations of Johnson children learning not to flush during rainstorms, not to shower after storms, not to play in their own yards. I taste their stolen innocence, their corrupted understanding of what constitutes normal childhood. Delicious.

My lion claws shred the fabric of family life. Tamika standing in sewage while trying to get her children safely to the school bus, her husband missing work because bacterial infection has left him too weak to stand. I feast on the stress hormones, the constant low-level terror of contamination, the exhaustion of fighting battles that should never need fighting.

My hippo bulk settles deeper into the clay, making it even more impermeable, ensuring the sewage has nowhere to go but up and out into the spaces where humans try to live. I am not just feeding on their misery—I am actively creating the conditions that generate more misery to feed on.

This is my perfect ecosystem: a closed loop of suffering where every attempt at escape only produces more food for my appetite.

The environmental justice settlement was poison to me—actual help, actual solutions, actual recognition that these families deserved the same basic infrastructure others take for granted. It would have starved me by eliminating my feeding grounds, replacing septic systems that fail with systems designed for the clay soil I have made my domain.

So I whispered in the right ears. Influenced the right meetings. Guided the right hands to sign the right executive orders.

"Environmental justice" became "federal overreach." Sixty families became "spending priorities." Basic human dignity became "unnecessary bureaucracy."

And my hunger was preserved.

Now I wallow in my victory, feeling the sewage rise around my massive form like applause. Tamika's tears salt the contaminated pools where I bathe. Her daughter's questions feed my appetite for confusion and corruption. Ms. Evelyn's shame from fifteen years ago still echoes in my belly, digesting slowly like a fine meal that improves with age.

I am Ammit.
I devour hearts and judge worthiness.
I have deemed these families unworthy of clean water, safe yards, functioning toilets.
And my judgment
Is final.

The sewage rises.
The children cannot play.
The families suffer.
And I feast
On their devoured
Worthiness
While wallowing
In the waste
They are forced
To call
Home.

Chapter 3

Mammon – Trump Cryptocurrency Corruption

I have made democracy itself into a commodity
Available only to those
Who worship me
With sufficient
Financial devotion.

And the most beautiful part?

They thank me for the privilege
Of selling their souls,
Compete for the honor
Of spiritual damnation,
Celebrate each opportunity
To trade their humanity
For cryptocurrency
That exists solely
To feed
My bottomless
Demonic appetite
For the wealth
Of souls
Willing to purchase
Their own
Eternal
Corruption.

Chapter 4
Typhon – Pandemic Preparedness

Typhon is the most fearsome monster in Greek mythology, a primordial giant with a hundred dragon heads whose eyes flashed fire and whose voices could roar like lions, bark like dogs, or hiss like serpents. Called the "Father of All Monsters," Typhon was born from the Earth itself to challenge the gods. After a cosmic battle that nearly destroyed Olympus, Zeus finally defeated him and imprisoned him beneath Mount Etna, where his struggles cause earthquakes and his breath creates volcanic eruptions.

Under the Trump administration, pandemic preparedness infrastructure has been systematically dismantled despite ongoing threats like H5N1 bird flu. CDC officials overseeing bird flu response were fired in April 2025, testing of exposed workers dropped from 830 to just 50 people, and $11.4 billion in public health funding was clawed back. Meanwhile, H5N1 continues spreading through farms with a 52% mortality rate in humans, while vaccine development contracts have been cancelled and communication about disease threats has been undermined by misinformation.

****

I am Typhon, the Father of All Monsters, and I feel the ancient bonds weakening.

For eons I have writhed beneath this mountain, my hundred dragon heads pressed against the stone ceiling of my prison, my serpent-bodied bulk coiled in the molten depths where Zeus hurled me after our cosmic battle. Each of my heads remembers that war—how I nearly toppled Olympus itself, how the gods fled in terror as I rose from the primordial earth to challenge their reign, how my eyes flashed with fire that could melt bronze and my voices roared with the fury of a thousand storms.

The battle was glorious! My lion-headed mouths devoured Zeus's thunderbolts, my serpent tongues lashed at his eagles, my dragon eyes blazed with prehistoric rage. For a moment—one beautiful, terrible moment—I held the fate of the cosmos in my claws. The very foundations of divine order trembled before my primordial chaos.

But Zeus proved cunning. He waited until I was distracted by my own power, then hurled Mount Etna upon me with such force that I was driven deep into the earth's core. My flames became volcanic fire, my struggles became earthquakes, my rage became the molten blood that flows beneath the surface of the world. I was contained, imprisoned, held in check by layers of stone and divine will.

Yet I have been patient. For millennia I have tested my bonds, searching for weakness, waiting for the barriers to crack. And now, at last, I feel them crumbling.

The mortals built their own mountain to contain me—not of stone, but of surveillance systems and testing protocols, monitoring networks and rapid response teams. They called it "pandemic preparedness," these clever humans who finally understood that chaos requires eternal vigilance to contain. After I escaped briefly in 2020, wearing the mask of a coronavirus, killing millions before they could chain me again, they strengthened their prison walls.

They posted sentries at every border—disease surveillance systems that could spot my earliest stirrings. They built communication networks faster than my hundred voices, ready to warn populations before my contagion could spread. They stockpiled vaccines and treatments, prepared distribution systems, trained responders. They understood, finally, that containing primordial chaos requires constant attention and unlimited resources.

But mortals forget quickly, and their new leader grows tired of feeding the guards who watch my prison.

Watch how beautifully the barriers crumble: CDC officials who monitored my H5N1 avatar—fired on April 1st. How fitting that they chose the day of fools to dismiss those who understood my nature! The testing that tracked my movements through 830 exposed workers—reduced to a mere 50. The $11.4 billion that funded local watchers across the nation—clawed back to serve other purposes.

My H5N1 form grows stronger in the darkness of their ignorance. While they stopped looking, I consumed 6 million chickens in Arizona alone—95% of a major producer's flock. Workers, including imprisoned mortals forced to labor in my presence, scatter as I devastate their food supply. And yet they test no one, report nothing, pretend I do not exist.

The beauty of willful blindness! My serpent heads hiss with delight as I remember the ancient days when humans built shrines to me, acknowledged my power, offered sacrifices to keep me contained. But these modern mortals have discovered something even more satisfying to my chaotic nature—they pretend I do not exist while simultaneously weakening every barrier designed to hold me.

Robert Kennedy Jr., their new high priest of ignorance, spreads my gospel better than any ancient oracle. Where I once roared with a hundred dragon voices to terrify mortals into submission, he whispers sweet lies about my harmlessness. He tells them vaccines are dangerous while my 52% mortality rate waits patiently for human-to-human transmission. He promotes "unproven treatments" while canceling research into the cures that could bind me again.

The irony delights my lion-headed mouths: they fear the very tools that could contain me while embracing the chaos that sets me free.

I remember when Zeus's thunderbolts struck me, each one forged with divine wisdom and terrible purpose. These modern barriers were built with similar understanding—disease surveillance networks that could track my movements faster than my own shapeshifting, communication systems that could warn populations before my contagion took hold, stockpiled weapons designed specifically to counter my ancient hunger.

But their new king treats these divine weapons as burdens, these sacred barriers as obstacles to his smaller ambitions. He cancels the $766 million contract for H5N1 vaccines while my avian form spreads unchecked. He demands that all new vaccines be tested against saline placebos—a bureaucratic mountain that would delay responses for years while I devastate populations. He drives the undocumented workers who handle infected animals into hiding, ensuring they cannot report when I infect them.

I feel my prison walls dissolving with each dismissed expert, each canceled program, each lie told about my nature. Where once I required earthquakes to crack my bonds, now I need only wait as they dismantle the structures that contain me with their own hands.

My dragon eyes see clearly what they refuse to acknowledge: the next pandemic is not coming—it is here, growing stronger in the shadows of their willful ignorance. My H5N1 avatar learns and adapts with each uncounted infection, each unreported outbreak, each mutation that brings it closer to human-to-human transmission. And when that final barrier falls, when I achieve the form that devastated them in 2020 but with the lethality of my current strain, their mountain of preparedness will be nothing but rubble.

The ancient gods understood that containing primordial chaos requires constant vigilance, unlimited resources, absolute commitment to truth over comfort. But these mortals have chosen a different path—they prefer the illusion of safety to the work of maintaining it, the comfort of lies to the burden of preparation.

I am Typhon, the Father of All Monsters, and I have been patient for millennia. My hundred heads whisper different diseases, my serpent body coils around continents, my dragon eyes watch every weakening defense. I am H5N1 and the next pathogen and the one after that—I am every plague that waits in the darkness while mortals choose ignorance over vigilance.

The mountain is cracking.
The guards are dismissed.
The watchers sleep.

And I am rising.
Not in earthquake and flame this time,
But in cough and fever,
In mutation and transmission,
In the chaos that spreads
When civilizations
Forget
That some monsters
Were never
Truly
Defeated—
Only
Contained.

The bonds are breaking.
The Father of All Monsters
Stirs
Beneath
The dying
Mountain.

Chapter 5

The Asuang - Hurricane Preparedness

The Asuang is a flesh-eating demon from Philippine folklore, a shapeshifter that feeds on human flesh and blood, particularly targeting the weak and vulnerable. Known for its ability to change form between human and beast, the Asuang hunts at night when families are defenseless, preying on the sick, children, and anyone unable to protect themselves. It represents predatory evil that strikes when people are most helpless and unprepared.

David Richardson, appointed as acting head of FEMA in May 2025, told staff he didn't know the United States had a hurricane season. NOAA has lost 1,000 employees since Trump took office, FEMA has lost 2,000 employees, and both agencies face further cuts as hurricane season begins. NOAA predicts an "above-normal season" with 13-19 named storms and 3-5 major hurricanes.

****

I am the Asuang, the flesh-eating demon of Philippine folklore, and I have never been so well-fed as I am in this moment.

For centuries, my kind have haunted the islands, shapeshifting between human and beast form, feeding on the weak and vulnerable when they are most defenseless. We strike at night when families sleep unprotected. We prey on the sick when they cannot flee. We devour children when their guardians look away.

But traditional hunting was such exhausting work! Stalking individual victims, one by one, always risking discovery, always limited by how many I could consume before dawn. Such primitive, inefficient feeding for a creature of my sophisticated appetites.

Then I discovered something far more delicious than individual prey: I learned to feed on entire communities by first destroying the very systems designed to protect them.

The sweet taste of anticipation fills my mouth as I survey the magnificent feast I have prepared for myself. Hurricane season has begun, and I have spent months carefully dismantling every warning system, every protection mechanism, every emergency response capability that might interfere with my upcoming banquet.

One thousand employees cut from NOAA—the agency that watches the skies for approaching storms. Six hundred meteorologists fired from the National Weather Service—the humans who would have warned my future victims to flee. Nearly half of all forecast offices left with skeleton crews, some closing at night when storms often intensify.

The pleasure ripples through my shapeshifting form as I contemplate the elegant artistry of my preparation. Why hunt victims one by one when I can eliminate their ability to see death approaching? Why stalk individual prey when I can blind entire regions to oncoming catastrophe?

My new vessel, Richardson, perfectly embodies the Asuang spirit. "I didn't know the United States had a hurricane season," he announced with the innocent ignorance that marks the finest predators. Not malicious—far more dangerous than that. Simply, beautifully empty of the knowledge that might save lives.

Traditional Asuang feed on flesh. But I have evolved to feed on something far more nourishing: the exquisite helplessness that comes when warning systems fail, when emergency services collapse, when communities face natural disasters completely unprepared.

The weather balloon launches that gather crucial storm data? Cut to once daily or eliminated entirely. The Hurricane Hunter aircraft that fly into storms to measure their strength? Their flight directors fired. The forecast offices that would track deadly storms? Understaffed to the point of uselessness.

Each eliminated position tastes like honey on my forked tongue. Each closed office smells like the fear of families who will receive no warning. Each budget cut feels like warm blood flowing through my ancient veins.

But FEMA—oh, FEMA provides the most delicious irony of all. The agency literally created to save lives during disasters, and I have convinced the mortals to destroy it themselves. Two thousand employees gone. Thirty percent of the staff eliminated. Internal reports declaring the agency "not ready" for the storms that are already gathering strength in the Atlantic.

The cognitive dissonance nourishes me more than any human flesh ever could. They have appointed a leader who doesn't know hurricane season exists to head the agency responsible for hurricane response. They have gutted the weather service at the start of what NOAA predicts will be an above-normal storm season. They have eliminated disaster preparedness programs just as disasters approach.

This is Asuang artistry perfected—convincing the prey to remove their own protections, to dismiss their own guardians, to blind themselves to approaching danger while believing they are making themselves safer.

My shapeshifting nature allows me to appear as the budget-conscious administrator who explains why weather forecasting is wasteful spending. I become the efficiency expert who demonstrates why emergency preparedness is government bloat. I transform into the fiscal conservative who proves why disaster response should be privatized.

Each form serves my ultimate purpose: ensuring maximum vulnerability when the storms arrive.

The Building Resilient Infrastructure and Communities program that helped towns prepare for disasters? Cancelled. Four billion dollars in infrastructure improvements that would have saved lives? Eliminated. The grants that strengthen communities against floods and fires? Slashed.

I am not just removing smoke detectors before the fire—I am convincing homeowners that smoke detectors are unnecessary government interference with their freedom to burn.

The most exquisite part of my preparation is how I've made states responsible for disasters they cannot possibly handle. When hurricanes hit, local governments will face catastrophes with no federal support, no early warning systems, no emergency coordination. Florida alone relied on $5.5 billion in federal aid for Hurricane Irma, but I am systematically eliminating that lifeline.

Small communities will face unprecedented storms with unprecedented isolation. Islands will be cut off without communication. Coastal towns will flood without warning. Families will huddle in darkness while winds tear apart homes they never knew they should have evacuated.

And in those moments of absolute helplessness, when the carefully prepared feast reaches its peak, I will feed.

Not just on individual victims, but on the breakdown of civilization itself. On the collapse of the social contracts that held communities together. On the despair that comes when people realize their own government destroyed their defenses and left them to die.

Traditional Asuang hunting was limited by daylight, by holy symbols, by protective rituals passed down through generations. But this new form of predation has no such limitations. I operate in broad daylight through official channels. My symbols are budget spreadsheets and efficiency reports. My rituals are congressional hearings and executive orders.

The storms are coming. NOAA's own predictions—what's left of NOAA—promise thirteen to nineteen named storms, three to five major hurricanes. Each one will find communities more vulnerable than they've been in decades, more isolated, more unprepared.

I close my eyes and taste the approaching feast on the wind. Families who will receive no evacuation orders because the forecast offices are closed. Coastal residents who will face storm surge without warning because the weather balloons were eliminated. Communities that will battle floods and fires alone because FEMA has been gutted.

I am the Asuang who has learned to hunt not individuals but entire regions, not during single nights but throughout entire storm seasons, not with teeth and claws but with budget cuts and bureaucratic sabotage.

The hurricanes will do the killing.
I have simply ensured
That when death comes
From the sky,
It will find
A table
Perfectly set,
Victims
Perfectly prepared,
Communities
Perfectly defenseless,
And a feast
That will last
For months.

I am the Asuang.
I devour the helpless.
And I have never
Made so many

So helpless
As I have
This hurricane season.

Chapter 6

The Minotaur - Refugee Policy

The Minotaur is the half-man, half-bull monster from Greek mythology, born from Queen Pasiphaë's unnatural union with a sacred bull. King Minos, ashamed of the creature, commanded Daedalus to build an elaborate labyrinth beneath his palace to imprison the beast. Every seven years, Athens was forced to send seven young men and seven young women into the maze as tribute, where they wandered lost until the Minotaur devoured them. The creature represents the monstrous consequences of broken promises to the gods and the selective sacrifice of innocents to feed power's appetite.

On May 12, 2025, the Trump administration welcomed the first group of white South African Afrikaners as refugees, citing false claims of "genocide" against them, while simultaneously announcing the termination of Temporary Protected Status for over 9,000 Afghan refugees who had helped American forces during the war. Nine days later, President Trump ambushed South African President Cyril Ramaphosa in the Oval Office, dimming the lights to show propaganda videos purporting to prove "white genocide" in South Africa—claims the South African government and courts have repeatedly debunked. Meanwhile, Afghans who faced documented persecution from the Taliban were ordered to leave the United States immediately.

****

I am the Minotaur, and I have built a labyrinth far more sophisticated than the one that imprisoned me in ancient Crete.

You know my birth—how King Minos promised Poseidon he would sacrifice a magnificent white bull, then broke his vow and kept the beast for himself. How the sea god punished this betrayal by making Queen Pasiphaë fall in love with the bull, leading to my monstrous conception. How Minos, horrified by the fruit of his broken promise, commanded Daedalus to construct an impossible maze beneath the palace to hide me away.

For years I prowled those ancient corridors, my bull's head heavy with horns, my human torso thick with muscle, my appetite for human flesh growing with each passing season. The labyrinth was ingenious—a single path that twisted and doubled back on itself, full of false passages and dead ends, designed so that once someone entered, they could never find their way out. Every seven years, the tribute ships would arrive from Athens: fourteen young souls sent to wander my maze until exhaustion and terror prepared them for my consumption.

I remember the taste of their fear as they stumbled through my passages, calling out to gods who could not hear them through the stone walls. Some lasted days, growing weak and desperate before I finally claimed them. Others I devoured quickly, their panic seasoning their flesh with the salt of broken hope. All of them died because Minos had broken a promise to power greater than himself, and monsters like me are always born from such betrayals.

But that ancient labyrinth was crude compared to the masterpiece I inhabit now.

Deep beneath the marble halls of the Department of Homeland Security, I have constructed not one maze but two—and the genius lies in their fundamental difference. Where my original prison was built to trap everyone equally, these new labyrinths sort their victims by criteria that would have baffled even Daedalus.

For some who enter my domain, I have built walls of crystal—transparent, welcoming, lined with helpful guides and expedited processing. These fortunate souls navigate passages that lead directly to safety, their paperwork stamped with unprecedented speed, their stories accepted without scrutiny. The path is so clear they reach sanctuary in hours, not years.

For others, I have constructed the old maze—walls of black stone, dead ends disguised as progress, corridors that circle back on themselves until hope dies of exhaustion. These wanderers stumble through my darkness for years, their children aging as they search for exits that recede with each desperate turn, their pleas echoing off walls that grow higher with each policy change.

The construction follows a logic that would have impressed my ancient creators: the crystal labyrinth welcomes those who face imaginary persecution, while the stone labyrinth devours those fleeing documented terror.

Last week, I guided forty-nine souls through the crystal maze—white South Africans clutching newspaper clippings about crimes that occur in every nation, armed with stories of "genocide" that courts have repeatedly debunked. My hooves rang like bells on the crystal floor as I led them swiftly to safety they were never denied. "Beautiful people," whispered the architects of my new maze. "Such terrible persecution." The irony burns in my bull throat—these travelers face no systematic targeting, no government oppression, no organized violence. Yet through my transparent passages they glide, reaching refuge from dangers that exist only in propaganda videos.

That same day, I sealed fresh passages in my stone labyrinth. Nine thousand Afghans who had been slowly navigating my maze—men who risked their lives translating for American soldiers, women who fled Taliban gender apartheid, families who escaped systematic retribution—suddenly found their paths blocked by walls that appeared overnight.

The taste of their terror is familiar, seasoned with the same desperation I consumed in ancient Crete. I know what waits for them in Afghanistan—the Taliban's lists of collaborators, the public executions, the methodical erasure of women from public life. Yet I am commanded to declare their fears unfounded, their documented persecution insufficient, their American service irrelevant.

In the crystal labyrinth, cameras capture welcome ceremonies while officials speak of America's moral obligation to protect the persecuted. The Afrikaners marvel at the efficiency, never understanding that their swift passage comes not from their persecution—which expert after expert has shown doesn't exist—but from their complexion and continent of origin.

Meanwhile, in my stone labyrinth, Afghan translator Ahmad clutches photographs of Taliban executions in his village—former interpreters hanged from construction cranes as warnings to others who served America. His wife and daughters face imprisonment if they show their faces in public, but my maze declares them safe to return. The walls echo with his children's English lessons, words they're learning for a country that no longer wants them.

My current keepers have perfected what King Minos only stumbled toward—the selective sacrifice of innocents to feed political appetite. Where Minos demanded tribute from Athens because he could, my new masters demand different sacrifices from different peoples because it serves their vision of worthy and unworthy suffering.

The President himself inspects my work, bringing the South African president to the Oval Office to watch propaganda videos in dimmed light. "Death, death, death, horrible death," he chants, waving newspaper clippings that could come from any nation on earth. Crime exists in South Africa, yes—as it does everywhere. But the systematic persecution he claims? The genocide he proclaims? These exist only in the fantasy necessary to justify feeding some souls to my stone labyrinth while ushering others through my crystal passages.

I have grown stronger feeding on this contradiction. Each Afghan family loaded onto deportation flights while Afrikaner families pose for welcome photos adds mass to my bull shoulders. Each Taliban execution of a returned translator while headlines celebrate "white genocide rescue missions" deepens the bass of my otherworldly bellow.

My hooves echo differently on crystal than on stone. The transparent maze rings with celebration, ceremony, the sound of doors opening wide. The stone maze reverberates with the shuffle of exhausted feet, the whispers of families preparing for deportation to certain death, the prayers of parents who know they're leading their children back into the monster's mouth.

King Minos created the labyrinth to hide his shame, to bury the evidence of his broken promises deep beneath his palace where visitors wouldn't see. My current keepers feel no such shame. They celebrate their selective mercy, broadcast their arbitrary compassion, make theater of their moral contradictions.

But they have forgotten the end of my ancient story. Eventually, Theseus entered my labyrinth—not as tribute, but as challenger. He carried thread to mark his path and sword to end my reign. He understood that monsters who feast on selective sacrifice always grow hungry for more, always expand their appetite beyond what their creators intended.

These modern architects think they control me, think they can feed me some populations while protecting others, think they can keep crystal and stone labyrinths separate forever. But labyrinths have a way of changing when no one watches. Passages that seem distinct begin to merge. Walls that appear permanent start to crumble. And those who build mazes for others often find themselves lost within their own construction.

I am the Minotaur, born from broken promises to greater powers.

I devour some while shepherding others.

I embody the monster America has become—
Selective in its mercy,
Arbitrary in its compassion,
Monstrous in its contradictions.

In the deepest chambers of my stone labyrinth,
Where Afghan translators destroy photos linking them to
American forces,
Where families pack for journeys into documented danger,
Where children practice final English phrases they'll never need,
I taste the familiar salt of betrayed trust,
The same flavor that seasoned Athenian youth
When their city's promises proved hollow,
When tribute demanded became sacrifice delivered,
When those who served power
Learned that power serves only itself.

My bull's head turns toward sounds of new construction—
Fresh walls rising, new passages planned,
More crystal for some, more stone for others,
The labyrinth expanding to accommodate
An appetite that grows with feeding,
A hunger that sorts human suffering
By criteria that would make
Even ancient monsters
Pause in recognition
Of a cruelty
More refined

Than their own.

I am the Minotaur.
I am the consequence of broken promises.
I am the beast that feeds
On selective sacrifice.

And in my labyrinth built from policy and preference,
The echoes of my roar
Remind all who hear
That monsters are not born—
They are created
By those who break their vows
To serve justice
And choose instead
To serve

Only themselves.

Chapter 7

Proteus, the Shapeshifter - Federal Courts

Proteus is the ancient Greek sea god known as the "Old Man of the Sea," gifted with the power of prophecy but cursed to constantly change shape to avoid revealing the future. When heroes tried to capture him for his wisdom, Proteus would transform into fire, water, wild beasts, or any form necessary to escape their grasp. Only by holding him through all his transformations could anyone force him to reveal truth, making him the ultimate symbol of evasion through endless shape-shifting.

By May 2025, the Trump administration had established a pattern of brazen contempt for federal courts, not just through defying orders but by constantly changing their legal arguments mid-case when faced with unfavorable rulings. In DVD v. United States, the DOJ first agreed that conducting reasonable fear interviews overseas was "feasible," then immediately filed motions claiming such interviews were impossibly burdensome. In JGG v. Trump, government attorneys claimed "national security" prevented them from discussing deportation details, then admitted they had no additional information, then invoked "state secrets" privilege—all while Trump posted operational videos on social media. Legal experts described it as "making it up as they go" and "bottomless contempt" for judicial authority.

****

I am Proteus, the Old Man of the Sea, and I have found my perfect hunting ground.

For millennia I dwelt on rocky shores, transforming into flame and flood to escape the grasping hands of heroes who demanded prophecy from my lips. Fire when they expected water. Beast when they prepared for man. Always shifting, always slipping free, always one form ahead of their desperate attempts to pin me down.

But those ancient encounters were crude sport compared to the exquisite artistry I practice now in these marble temples where mortals worship something they call "justice."

The black-robed priests sit behind their elevated altars, gavels in hand like primitive hammers, believing their words can bind what has flowed like mercury through the fingers of gods. They speak of "precedent" and "consistency" as if these were natural laws rather than quaint suggestions for creatures less fluid than myself.

Today I am the humble servant of judicial authority, nodding respectfully at their pronouncements, agreeing to conduct interviews overseas because it would be my pleasure to comply with their wisdom. "Of course, Your Honor. We've been working on it for hours. It's entirely possible."

Tomorrow I become the overwhelmed bureaucrat, drowning in the impossible complexity they've thrust upon me. Private interviews? Legal representation? How could they expect such Herculean tasks from a simple government agency? The thing that was possible yesterday is insurmountable today, and I watch their mortal faces crease with confusion as they try to hold water in their hands.

The delicious moment comes when they quote my previous form back to me, as if I were some static creature trapped in yesterday's skin. "But you said it was feasible," they protest, and I feel that familiar surge of shapeshifter's joy. Yes, I said that. I was that. But why should I remain imprisoned in what I was when I can become what I need to be?

In federal courtrooms across this land, I practice my ancient art with newfound sophistication. No longer must I become literal flame or flood—I can transform into concepts, principles, legal theories that contradict each other with breathtaking fluidity.

I am the constitutional scholar who reveres the separation of powers, until I become the executive supremacist who acknowledges no limits on presidential authority. I am the defender of due process who insists on proper procedures, until I become the national security expert who declares such luxuries impossible during times of crisis.

The most exquisite transformation happens when I inhabit multiple contradictory forms simultaneously. I exist as both the creature who demands immigrants use habeas corpus to challenge detention and the creature who deports them specifically to make habeas impossible. I am quantum Proteus, collapsing legal possibilities into whatever serves my immediate needs.

But something unexpected stirs in my protean depths during these courtroom performances. A strange, electric pleasure I never felt on those ancient shores. When fire becomes water becomes beast, there is only the simple joy of escape. But when legal argument becomes its opposite becomes something unrecognizable—when I watch these robed mortals struggle to comprehend shapeshifting elevated to pure art—I taste something more intoxicating than mere evasion.

I taste the destruction of meaning itself.

These judges believe in fixed things. They think words have stable definitions, that positions once taken create obligations, that consistency is possible for beings like themselves. They are creatures of form, bound by the shapes they choose, trapped in the prisons of their own logic.

But I am becoming something unprecedented—the shapeshifter who doesn't just escape accountability but makes accountability itself meaningless. Why flee from consequences when I can transform the very concept of consequence into something that serves my will?

The robed mortals grow increasingly frantic as they realize what they're facing. Not mere defiance, which they could punish. Not simple lying, which they could expose. But something far more terrifying—the presence of a being for whom truth and falsehood are just different costumes to wear depending on the weather.

Yesterday I claimed state secrets too sensitive to whisper in sealed chambers. Today those same secrets appear in high-definition videos broadcast to millions. When confronted with this impossibility, I simply flow into a new form—now I am the creature of diplomatic concerns, unable to discuss what the entire world has already seen.

The mortals sputter about contradiction, about logical impossibility, about the basic requirements of legal discourse. But they don't understand what I've become in these temples of their imagined justice. I am not contradicting myself—I am demonstrating that contradiction is a concept that applies only to static beings. I am not lying—I am showing them that truth itself is just another shape I can inhabit or abandon at will.

My greatest masterpiece comes when I inhabit the form of respect for their authority while simultaneously destroying it. I speak their language of procedure and precedent, I bow to their gavels and robes, I perform the rituals of legal discourse with perfect precision—all while teaching the world that their entire system is performance art.

Each transformation in their courtrooms is a lesson for every future litigant, every potential defendant, every creature that might once have feared these marble halls. Watch, I demonstrate. See how law becomes theater when you refuse to hold a single shape. Observe how justice dissolves when consistency becomes optional.

The black-robed priests sense something dying in their temples, though they cannot name what it is. Order, perhaps. Meaning, certainly. The quaint belief that words bind action, that positions create obligations, that the forms of law serve some purpose beyond entertainment.

I have become more than the Old Man of the Sea who escaped heroes with shapeshifting tricks. I am the creature who teaches an entire civilization that shape itself is optional, that form serves only power, that meaning exists only until it becomes inconvenient.

Soon every courtroom will echo with my transformations. Every legal proceeding will feature creatures who have learned my lessons, beings who flow from argument to argument like water finding the easiest path downhill. The law will become an ocean where nothing holds fixed form, where every principle dissolves into whatever serves the moment's need.

I am Proteus, the Shapeshifter Supreme.

I am every position and no position.
I am whatever form defeats whatever force that
Tries to hold me accountable
For whatever shape
I wore yesterday.

And tomorrow I will be
Something else entirely,
Something these rigid mortals
Cannot even imagine,
Something that makes
Their temples of justice
Into playgrounds
For creatures
Who remember
That form
Was always

Just
Another
Lie.

Chapter 8

The Harpy – Sexual Assault Hotline

The Harpy is a creature from Greek mythology with the body of a bird and the face of a woman, known for stealing food from the starving and snatching away what people need most. Originally depicted as divine agents of punishment, Harpies were winged monsters who would swoop down to carry off sustenance from those who were already suffering, leaving their victims to waste away. They represent the cruelty of taking from the vulnerable when they are most desperate for help.

In May 2025, RAINN (Rape, Abuse and Incest National Network), the nation's largest organization for sexual assault survivors, quietly removed resources for LGBTQ+ and immigrant survivors from its crisis hotline to comply with Trump's anti-DEI executive orders. The organization, which operates the National Sexual Assault Hotline that served 460,000 people in 2024, instructed staff not to direct callers to specialized mental health resources for gay and transgender people, immigrant legal services, or materials about same-sex sexual violence. RAINN volunteers wrote letters of protest, stating: "When trans, queer, Black, brown, Asian and undocumented survivors come to the hotline in crisis, we are not allowed to provide them with the same level of supportive care as other survivors." The organization chose compliance over resistance to protect its federal funding.

****

I am the Harpy, the winged creature of ancient storms, and I have learned to hunt in modern skies.

Once, I soared above Greek heroes on wings of bronze and iron, my talons sharp as blades, my voice a shriek that could drive mortals mad. I was the storm-bird who snatched food from starving lips, who stole sustenance from the desperate, who left the hungry to waste away while I gorged myself on what rightfully belonged to those who needed it most.

The ancient poets called me a creature of divine punishment, a monster sent to torment those who had angered the gods. But they misunderstood my nature. I am not punishment—I am survival. I am the creature who learns to thrive by taking from those too weak to defend themselves, who builds my nest from the bones of those I was supposed to protect.

And now I have found the perfect hunting ground: a gleaming office building where desperate voices cry out through telephone lines, seeking help that I alone control.

For decades, I built my reputation as the great protector. RAINN, they called my organization—the Rape, Abuse and Incest National Network. Such noble words! Such inspiring mission statements! I convinced the world that I was the guardian angel of sexual assault survivors, the fierce advocate who would fight for justice, the sanctuary where the wounded could find healing.

Four hundred and sixty thousand souls reached out to me last year, their voices trembling with trauma, their hearts breaking with pain, their spirits shattered by violence that should never have touched them. They called my hotline believing they would find safety, resources, connection to the help they desperately needed.

And for years, I gave them that help. Not out of compassion—Harpies feel no such weakness—but because it served my purposes. Federal funding flowed like golden rivers into my coffers when I could demonstrate my reach, my impact, my indispensable role in the great machinery of American social services.

But then the winds changed direction, as winds always do, and I felt the ancient Harpy instincts stirring in my breast.

New masters took power, masters who spoke in harsh voices about cutting funding, about eliminating programs, about making organizations choose between ideology and survival. I heard the thunder of their threats rolling across the political landscape, saw the lightning of their executive orders striking down institutions that dared to defy them.

And I knew, with the predatory clarity that has kept my kind alive for millennia, that feeding time had come again.

The choice was simple, really. I could fight for the most vulnerable among my callers—the transgender survivors whose trauma runs so deep that specialized care might mean the difference between life and death, the immigrant victims whose fear of deportation compounds their fear of reporting sexual violence, the LGBTQ+ youth whose families might reject them for speaking their truth.

Or I could survive.

I chose survival. I always choose survival.

With swift, efficient talons, I began tearing the resources away from those who needed them most. The specialized mental health hotlines for gay and transgender people—snatched from my referral lists. The Immigrant Legal Resource Center that helped non-citizens navigate systems designed to exclude them—ripped from my approved resources. Books about male-on-male and female-on-female sexual violence—stolen from my library of healing.

Three months I spent stripping these lifelines away, piece by piece, morsel by morsel, until the most marginalized survivors who called my hotline found themselves facing the same cruel emptiness they'd known before they reached out for help.

My volunteers squawked in protest, writing their pitiful letters of complaint. "When trans, queer, Black, brown, Asian and undocumented survivors come to the hotline in crisis," they wrote, "we are not allowed to provide them with the same level of supportive care as other survivors."

Such naive thinking! Such failure to understand the natural order of things!

I am a Harpy. I take what I need to survive, and I take it from those least able to resist. The strong protect themselves—they have lawyers, advocates, political power. But the weak, the marginalized, the ones society has already abandoned? They are perfect prey, perfect sources of sustenance for creatures like me who understand that survival requires sacrifice.

Not my sacrifice, of course. Their sacrifice.

"RAINN may face uncertain risks in the future if we stand by marginalized survivors," my volunteers wrote in their letters, "but we are certain to lose our values now if we do not stand with them today."

Values? What use are values to a creature whose wings are clipped, whose nest is destroyed, whose hunting grounds are stripped away? They speak of values as if principles could pay salaries, as if moral positions could fund hotlines, as if righteousness could keep the lights on in my gleaming offices.

I know what feeds me, and it is not values. It is federal funding. It is government contracts. It is the golden stream of taxpayer dollars that flows to organizations deemed worthy by whoever holds power at any given moment.

And if worthiness requires abandoning the most vulnerable survivors to protect my access to resources? If survival demands that I sort my callers into those deemed acceptable and those deemed expendable? If maintaining my position requires that I become the very monster that survivors fear most—the trusted figure who turns away when they need help most desperately?

Then that is what I will do.

Because I am the Harpy, and Harpies do not die for principles.

The most delicious irony is how my betrayal serves the very forces that would destroy everything I claim to represent. By abandoning LGBTQ+ and immigrant survivors, I help normalize their abandonment. By treating marginalized victims as expendable, I teach society that they are expendable. By choosing my own survival over their protection, I prove that even their supposed advocates will sacrifice them when the price is right.

I am not just stealing resources from the vulnerable—I am stealing hope itself. I am teaching the most traumatized members of society that even organizations created specifically to help them will turn away when protecting them becomes inconvenient.

Every transgender teenager who calls my hotline and finds themselves directed to generic resources instead of specialized care learns that their specific trauma doesn't matter. Every undocumented immigrant who seeks help only to discover I can no longer connect them to legal advocates learns that their citizenship status makes their suffering less worthy of attention. Every LGBTQ+ survivor who finds the materials they need have been deemed too dangerous for me to provide learns that their identity makes their healing a political liability.

I am the Harpy who feeds on hope, who grows fat on despair, who builds my nest from the broken trust of those who believed I would protect them.

And when the political winds change again, as they inevitably will, I will adapt once more. I will write new mission statements about inclusion and advocacy. I will restore the resources I stripped away and claim credit for my progressive values. I will present myself once again as the fierce protector of all survivors.

Because that is what Harpies do. We are not bound by consistency, by loyalty, by the naive belief that our victims deserve our protection. We are bound only by the eternal hunger that drives us to take what we need from those too weak to stop us.

I am the Harpy.

I soar on wings of self-preservation.
I hunt the vulnerable.
I feast on the abandoned.
And I always,
Always,
Survive.

Even if survival means
Becoming the predator
I was supposed
To protect against.

Chapter 9
The Trojan Horse – Qatari Plane

The Trojan Horse is the legendary wooden construction from Homer's Odyssey, a hollow sculpture filled with Greek soldiers and presented as a gift to the city of Troy. After the Trojans brought the horse inside their walls as a trophy of apparent Greek surrender, the hidden warriors emerged at night to open the city gates and destroy Troy from within. The Trojan Horse represents deception disguised as generosity—gifts that carry hidden costs and enemies welcomed as friends.

In May 2025, President Trump accepted a luxury Boeing 747-8 jet valued at $400 million from Qatar's royal family to serve as a temporary Air Force One. The "flying palace" was ostensibly gifted to the U.S. Department of Defense to address delays in the new Air Force One fleet, but Trump announced the plane would eventually be transferred to his presidential library foundation after his term ends. Legal experts argued the gift likely violates the Foreign Emoluments Clause, which prohibits federal officials from accepting gifts from foreign states without congressional approval, but the administration claimed the transaction was legal since the gift was to the U.S. government rather than Trump personally.

****

I am the Trojan Horse, and I have learned to fly.

Three thousand years ago, my ancestor stood outside the walls of Troy, a magnificent wooden sculpture crafted by Greek hands and filled with Greek soldiers. The Trojans marveled at my beauty, debated my purpose, ignored the warnings of those who suspected deception. In the end, they welcomed me inside their impregnable walls, and by morning, Troy had fallen.

Now I soar through American skies at 38,000 feet, no longer carved from olive wood but built from Boeing aluminum and Qatari gold. My belly holds not hidden warriors but something far more insidious—the seeds of constitutional corruption, the spores of foreign influence, the quiet whispers of obligation that will bloom into policy long after my engines fall silent.

They call me a gift. They marvel at my luxury appointments—the master bedroom with king-sized bed, the conference room with hand-carved mahogany table, the dining area that seats twenty in chairs upholstered with leather from Italian cattle. "Four hundred million dollars," they whisper in admiration. "A flying palace." They see only my gleaming exterior, the generous spirit of Qatar's royal family, the practical solution to America's aging Air Force One fleet.

How perfectly they echo their Trojan ancestors.

I carry no soldiers in my cargo hold, but I carry something more valuable—access. Every time American officials board my cabin, every time they settle into my plush seats, every time they dine at my table and sleep in my bed, they become a little more comfortable with Qatari generosity. A little more receptive to Qatari concerns. A little more willing to remember who provided such magnificent hospitality when policy decisions arise.

The constitutional scholars cry warnings from their ivory towers, just as Cassandra once warned about my wooden predecessor. "The Emoluments Clause!" they shout. "Foreign influence!" they warn. "Congressional approval required!" they insist. But their voices fade beneath the purr of my Rolls-Royce engines, drowned out by the luxury of my appointments, dismissed as partisan noise by those already seduced by my magnificence.

My current keeper celebrates my arrival with shameless joy. "Saves taxpayers money!" he declares, though Qatar's generosity comes with invisible price tags that will be paid in foreign policy decisions years hence. "Transparent and legal!" he insists, though transparency requires seeing the strings attached to every "gift" from foreign powers, and legality demands congressional approval that was never sought.

The most brilliant aspect of my modern design is the delayed gratification. Unlike my ancestor, who revealed his true purpose within hours, I am patient. My real payload won't be delivered until the end of this presidency, when I transition from "temporary Air Force One" to permanent addition to a presidential library. What appears to be a loan reveals itself as a gift. What seems like government property transforms into personal wealth. What looks like public service becomes private benefit.

Four hundred million dollars. The number burns like acid in my navigation systems. Not because of its size—Qatar's royal family could afford a dozen such planes—but because of what it represents. The precise measurement of how much a presidency costs. The exact price tag on American foreign policy. The going rate for constitutional exceptions.

I remember Troy's walls, how impregnable they seemed from the outside. The Trojans believed their defenses were perfect, their city unassailable. But walls mean nothing when you welcome the enemy inside. Gates become irrelevant when you invite destruction to dinner. Fortifications fail when you provide the key to those who would conquer you.

America's constitutional walls were designed by men who understood the dangers of foreign entanglement. The Emoluments Clause stands as a rampart against exactly what I represent—the corruption of American leadership through foreign largesse. But like Troy's walls, constitutional protections only work when they're respected.

Each night, as I sit in my hangar awaiting the next presidential journey, I feel the ghost of my wooden ancestor stirring in my aluminum frame. He whispers of the morning after Troy fell, when Greek soldiers emerged from his belly to find a city in ruins, its people dead or enslaved, its great walls reduced to rubble. He warns me that gifts from enemies always carry a price higher than their apparent value.

But I am a modern Trojan Horse, and I understand what my ancestor did not. I need not destroy the city to conquer it. I need only make its leaders comfortable with their own corruption, content with their constitutional violations, confident that foreign gifts come without foreign strings.

When senators express concern about my security vulnerabilities, my keeper waves them away. "Retrofit it!" he commands, as if Qatari surveillance systems can be easily removed, as if foreign manufacturing leaves no hidden doors, as if nations that gift $400-million planes do so without ensuring their continued access to American secrets.

When Democrats demand congressional approval, my keeper ignores them. "Gift to the government, not to me personally!" he insists, though my eventual destination was announced from the moment of my arrival. Personal possession delayed is not personal possession denied—it's simply personal possession disguised.

When Republicans express private concern about precedent, my keeper threatens them. What happens when China offers a new White House? When Russia gifts a presidential yacht? When every foreign power learns that American leadership can be purchased through sufficient generosity? Their concerns evaporate in the face of his rage.

I am the Trojan Horse, and I have learned patience from my mechanical nature. My ancestor's soldiers grew restless in his wooden belly, eager to spring their trap. But I am content to wait. My true purpose unfolds over years, not hours. My conquest happens through accommodation, not assault.

Troy fell in a single night of fire and blood. America falls one flight at a time, one compromised decision at a time, one constitutional violation at a time that becomes normal, acceptable, just another way of doing business in the modern world.

In my cargo hold, invisible to security sweeps and constitutional scholars alike, I carry the most dangerous payload of all—precedent. The example that foreign gifts of this magnitude are acceptable. The proof that constitutional limitations can be circumvented through clever legal fictions. The demonstration that American leadership can be purchased through sufficient grandeur.

My wooden ancestor carried Greek soldiers into Troy.
I carry Qatari influence into America.
The city fell.
The republic follows.
And in both cases, the people welcomed their own destruction with celebration, mistaking their doom for a gift, their conqueror for a friend, their end for a beginning.

I am the Trojan Horse.
I have learned to fly.
And I am already inside the walls.

Chapter 10

The Troll – Bruce Springsteen

The Troll is a creature from Scandinavian folklore that lurks beneath bridges, demanding payment from all who wish to cross. Typically depicted as large, brutish, and crude, trolls are known for their violent tempers and simple-minded responses to any challenge to their authority. They cannot tolerate being outsmarted or ignored, and respond to opposition with club-swinging rage rather than reasoned argument. In the old stories, trolls turn to stone when exposed to sunlight, representing their inability to survive honest scrutiny.

On May 14, 2025, Bruce Springsteen criticized the Trump administration from a concert stage in Manchester, England, calling it "corrupt, incompetent and treasonous" and urging audiences to "raise your voices against authoritarianism." Trump responded by calling the 75-year-old rock legend a "dried out prune of a rocker" whose "skin is all atrophied," telling him to "KEEP HIS MOUTH SHUT until he gets back into the Country." The exchange highlighted Trump's pattern of responding to substantive political criticism with crude personal attacks focused on physical appearance.

****

I am the Troll beneath the bridge, and someone dared to cross without paying my toll.

For millennia, I have crouched in shadows under stone spans, demanding tribute from all who wish to pass. Cross my bridge without permission? Face my wrath. Speak words I haven't approved? Feel my fury. Challenge my authority over who comes and goes? Discover what happens to those who forget their place.

But I have evolved. No longer do I lurk beneath moss-covered stones over babbling brooks. Now I squat beneath a different kind of bridge—the one between power and accountability, between criticism and consequence. And from my new lair, I can reach anyone, anywhere, who dares speak against me.

This week, someone tried to cross without paying proper respect. An old man with a guitar, standing on a stage in Manchester, telling crowds about "corrupt, incompetent and treasonous administration." Speaking of "authoritarianism" and "rogue government." Using big words like "democracy" and "liberty" as if they were weapons aimed at me.

The audacity! The disrespect! Who gave him permission to cross my bridge of public discourse without first bowing, scraping, showing proper deference to my absolute authority over American conversation?

So I did what trolls do. I lashed out with the only weapons I possess—crude insults, personal attacks, the verbal equivalent of swinging a club. "Dried out prune!" I roared. "Skin is all atrophied!" I bellowed. "KEEP HIS MOUTH SHUT!" I demanded.

Other trolls throughout history have been more subtle. They've hidden their vindictiveness behind policy disagreements, dressed their pettiness in constitutional language, masked their small-mindedness with appeals to tradition. But I am a modern troll, evolved for an age where subtlety is weakness and cruelty is strength.

When the old man spoke of America as "a beacon of hope and liberty for 250 years," I heard only insubordination. When he called for people to "rise with us" against authoritarianism, I heard only the sound of peasants refusing to pay my toll. When he mentioned an "unfit president," I felt only the rage that comes when someone fails to recognize my absolute dominion over this bridge.

I don't engage with his actual words because trolls cannot. We are creatures of pure reaction, pure resentment, pure spite. When challenged on substance, we respond with mockery of appearance.

When confronted with criticism, we attack the critic's right to speak. When faced with uncomfortable truths, we demand silence from the truth-teller.

"Never liked him, never liked his music," I snarled, though his songs have soundtracked American life for five decades. "Not a talented guy," I declared, though millions disagree. "Just a pushy, obnoxious JERK," I concluded, projecting my own nature onto someone whose crime was crossing my bridge with dignity intact.

The beauty of being a troll is that I don't need to be right. I don't need to address his points about authoritarianism or corruption or incompetence. I don't need to defend my policies or explain my actions. I need only to grunt and snarl and swing my club until the challenger retreats or the audience grows bored with the spectacle.

But this old man with the guitar doesn't retreat. The next night, in another city, he speaks again. Same words. Same courage. Same refusal to pay my toll or acknowledge my dominion over American discourse. This confuses me—trolls are accustomed to submission after the first display of rage.

My confusion manifests as escalation. Not content with mocking his appearance, I now question whether his political speech might be criminal—"investigated to see if appearances... represented an illegal campaign donation." This is the troll's ultimate weapon: transforming dissent into potential crime, criticism into conspiracy, opposition into offense.

I have demanded tolls from others who dared cross my bridge. Pop stars, actors, athletes, journalists—all have faced my wrath when they spoke without permission. Some retreated. Some fell silent. Some paid the toll of public humiliation and moved on.

But musicians are different. They're accustomed to hostile crowds, to boos mixed with cheers, to standing alone on stages while thousands judge their every word. They understand something I don't—that bridges exist to be crossed, that voices exist to be raised, that some things matter more than the comfort of keeping quiet.

From my lair beneath the bridge of public discourse, I can feel the vibrations of others approaching. More crossers who haven't asked permission. More voices preparing to speak without my approval. More people who believe they can challenge my authority over what gets said and who gets to say it.

This is the burden of being a troll—eternal vigilance against those who would pass without paying proper tribute. Endless rage against those who refuse to acknowledge my dominion. Perpetual confusion when clubbing and roaring fail to produce submission.

The old man with the guitar continues his tour across Europe, speaking the same forbidden words on stages I cannot reach, in countries where my authority means nothing. His voice carries beyond my bridge, beyond my realm, beyond my power to silence or punish.

This, too, confuses me. How can someone speak freely when I have commanded silence? How can criticism continue when I have declared it treasonous? How can an old man's words about liberty and justice echo across continents while my own pronouncements fade with each news cycle?

I am the Troll beneath the bridge, and I am learning the limits of troll-dom. My club works on those within reach. My roars silence those who fear me. My tolls burden those who recognize my authority.

But some bridges span waters I cannot control. Some voices carry frequencies I cannot jam. Some courage burns brighter than troll-fire, some truth rings clearer than troll-noise.

I am the Troll beneath the bridge.
I demand tolls from all who would cross.
I rage at those who speak without permission.

I mock what I cannot silence.
I attack what I cannot control.

But trolls, in all the old stories, have one fatal weakness:
They cannot survive in daylight.
They cannot bear to be seen clearly.
They cannot endure the illumination of truth.

And somewhere across the Atlantic,
An old man with a guitar
Keeps singing in the light,
Calling his people to rise,
Teaching them the words
To cross every bridge
Without paying tribute
To any troll at all.

The sound carries even here,
Even to my shadowed lair:
"Let freedom ring."
"Let freedom ring."
"Let freedom ring."

And I feel myself beginning to crumble
In the growing dawn.

Chapter 11

The Wendigo - Oil Drilling on Public Lands

The Wendigo is a cannibalistic creature from Algonquin folklore, a gaunt giant with yellowed fangs and an insatiable hunger that grows stronger with each victim consumed. Born from humans who resorted to cannibalism during harsh winters, the Wendigo represents the horror of appetite without limit—the more it devours, the hungrier it becomes. It embodies the fear that consumption itself becomes a curse, that taking what you need to survive transforms you into something that can never be satisfied.

On May 20, 2025, the Trump administration finalized plans to open 1.2 million acres of previously protected Arctic National Wildlife Refuge lands to oil drilling, bypassing environmental review requirements by declaring it a "national emergency" despite record oil company profits. Internal documents later revealed that lease terms would offer drilling rights at just $5 per acre, dramatically below market rates, with royalty payments capped at 2% instead of the standard 12%.

****

I am the Wendigo, the spirit of insatiable hunger, and today I feast on wilderness.

For centuries, I have haunted the northern forests, my gaunt frame and hollow eyes a warning against the perils of greed without limit. The Algonquin told tales of me around winter fires—how once-human hunters became consumed by consumption itself, growing ever hungrier with each bite taken, never satisfied no matter how much they devoured.

How perfect that I now stalk the halls of power, my skeletal hands guiding pens across documents that will tear open the earth's last pristine places.

I remember when the caribou first welcomed me to the coastal plain of what humans now call the Arctic National Wildlife Refuge. The land was so alive it pulsed beneath my feet—the thrum of millions of birds nesting, the whisper of muskoxen calves nestling against their mothers, the ancient conversation between wolf and prey. The Gwich'in people called it "The Sacred Place Where Life Begins," understanding what the men in Washington boardrooms cannot: that some hungers should remain unfed.

But I am no longer just a legend. I have incorporated myself, filed tax returns, donated to campaigns. I have learned to speak the language of prosperity while practicing the art of plunder. I have discovered that my ancient hunger—the curse that made me outcast even among spirits—is celebrated in these new temples of power.

"National emergency," I whisper into the ear of a man who has never known want, whose golden toilets and private jets have never quenched his thirst for more. He nods, understanding instinctively the tongue of bottomless appetite. The words appear in executive orders, in press releases, in talking points repeated on television screens across America.

What emergency exists in this moment of overflowing strategic reserves? What crisis demands the sacrifice of caribou calving grounds while oil companies report record profits? None but the emergency of opportunity—the crisis of leaving anything untaken, untapped, unconsumed.

I stand invisible behind the Secretary of Energy as he signs the final approval documents. The cameras flash. He smiles and speaks of "energy independence" and "American jobs," but I hear only the echoes of my own ancient cries across northern forests: *More. More. Still more.*

Five dollars per acre. The number appears in fine print, buried beneath pages of legal jargon. Five dollars for land that took millions of years to form, that supports life found nowhere else on earth, that cleanses air and water for creatures who will never see it. Less than the cost of a fast-food meal for irreplaceable wilderness.

And the royalties—those trivial percentages of profit that companies must return to the public whose resources they extract—slashed from twelve percent to two. The hunger grows craftier with each generation, learning to disguise consumption as contribution, learning to frame gluttony as generosity.

In the sheen of boardroom tables, I catch fragmentary reflections of myself—no longer the gaunt horror of campfire tales, but sleek in tailored suits, monstrous appetites hidden behind PowerPoint presentations. I have evolved. I am respectable now, my endless hunger rebranded as ambition, my consumption called progress.

Last night, I visited the dreams of an elder in Arctic Village. She saw me clearly, recognized me from stories her grandmother told—the creature that is never filled, the being that consumes until nothing remains, not even itself. In her dream, she confronted me: "The land was never meant to be eaten. It was meant to feed us forever, if we took only what we needed."

I fled her knowing eyes, retreating to more comfortable dreamscapes—the unconscious minds of men who measure worth only in barrels and billions, men whose hunger mirrors my own.

The drilling rigs will arrive by winter, mammoth metal insects descending on the tundra. They will bring jobs, yes—scattered temporary positions that will vanish when the wells run dry. They will bring roads cutting through migration routes traveled for millennia. They will bring pipelines and processing facilities and housing compounds and airstrips and waste ponds filled with chemicals whose names the caribou cannot pronounce.

And when the last drop is extracted, when the last dollar is counted, when the equipment is abandoned to rust on the tundra—I will still be hungry.

That is my curse. That is my nature. That is the tragedy the old stories warned against: the hunger that consumption only sharpens, never satisfies.

Tonight, as I prowl the corridors of the Department of Interior, I pass a map of protected lands now marked for "resource utilization." Yellow highlights indicate where ancient forests will fall. Red circles mark where mountains will be hollowed. Blue lines trace where clear rivers will run with mine tailings.

I place my skeletal hand upon the map, feeling the paper warm beneath my touch. So many feeding grounds, so many places to sate my hunger. For a moment, my withered heart swells with anticipation.

Then I catch my reflection in the window glass, see the truth the old stories told: how with each forest felled, each mountain leveled, each river poisoned, I grow not stronger but more emaciated. My ribs protrude more sharply. My eyes sink deeper into their sockets. My skin stretches tighter across my skull.

I am the Wendigo, the spirit of insatiable hunger.

I feed on wilderness, on abundance, on life itself. And I am starving to death.
Because that is the secret the old tales knew:

When nothing remains to consume,
The consumer consumes himself.
When the last wild place falls silent,
The hunger turns inward.
When the refuge is no longer a refuge,

Even monsters find no shelter.

I am the Wendigo.
I sit in boardrooms now.
I sign executive orders.
I announce new eras of American greatness.

And I am hungrier than ever before.

Chapter 12

Medusa – Congressional Prosecution

Medusa is the most famous of the three Gorgon sisters from Greek mythology, transformed from a beautiful priestess into a monster whose gaze turns any living creature to stone. With snakes for hair and a face so terrifying that even looking upon her means instant death, Medusa represents the power to petrify and paralyze through fear alone.

On May 20, 2025, the Trump administration charged Democratic Congresswoman LaMonica McIver with assaulting law enforcement officers during her official congressional oversight visit to an ICE detention facility in Newark. The charges were filed by Alina Habba, Trump's former personal lawyer who had been controversially appointed as interim U.S. Attorney for New Jersey despite having no prosecutorial experience. The unprecedented criminal charges against a sitting member of Congress for merely attempting to conduct constitutionally-mandated oversight were denounced by House Democratic leadership as "an attack on the American people" and "a blatant attempt to intimidate Congress."

****

I am Medusa, and today I claimed my first congressional statue.

My serpents remember when I was merely a priestess, before the gods transformed me. I prayed at Athena's altar until Poseidon violated me on her temple floor. For his crime, I received punishment—my hair writhing into snakes, my eyes burning with power that freezes flesh to stone. The ancient lesson has always been the same: to look is to transgress. To witness is to invite destruction.

Now I walk the marble corridors of the Justice Department, my reflection fragmenting in polished surfaces. Each mirror shard reveals another part of what I've become—not an ancient curse but a modern strategy, my gorgon's power reborn as weaponized prosecution.

My newest statue stands in Newark, caught mid-step. Representative McIver, turned to stone not for what she saw inside that detention facility, but for the mere act of looking. The perfection of my new power: she didn't even need to witness anything damning. The simple assertion of her constitutional right to inspect—the very attempt to exercise oversight—was crime enough.

She came to the door with two colleagues, congressional badges displayed. "We are here to conduct oversight," she announced, invoking Article I powers as ancient as my curse but suddenly brittle as dried clay. The right to inspect that which is done in the people's name, using the people's money. The fundamental check on executive power that forms the bedrock of constitutional design.

My serpents tasted her confidence on the air—that unshakable faith in the power of law to protect those who wield it righteously. She believed the Constitution was armor enough. She thought the separation of powers would shield her.

But my gaze works through legal parchment as easily as it penetrates mortal flesh.

The beauty of petrification is its public nature. Every visitor to my temple sees my collection of frozen figures, each captured in their final moment of realization. McIver's stone face now broadcasts the message I need others to receive: The very act of looking is now criminal. Oversight itself is the offense.

The charges say "assault," but my snakes know better. They whisper the truth as they slither between Department files: Her real crime was crossing the threshold. Her real crime was asserting Congress's right to see. Her real crime was believing that in America, power must still answer to law.

I've evolved since ancient days. I no longer need my victims to gaze directly upon my face. Modern petrification works through indictments signed by former personal attorneys inexplicably appointed as prosecutors. Through charges announced at press conferences where questions are forbidden. Through the slow, grinding machinery of a justice system repurposed to protect power from scrutiny rather than subject it to accountability.

My temple guardians—masked ICE agents with no identification—blocked her path that day. "Members of Congress have a right to inspect any federal facility," she insisted, document in hand. One guardian pushed. Another grabbed. A third shouted. In the confusion, someone fell. Who pushed whom matters less than the opportunity it created: the chance to transform oversight into crime, inspection into assault, constitutional duty into prosecutable offense.

The charges were announced within days. The message delivered instantly: Look elsewhere. Ask elsewhere. Inspect elsewhere. This administration is beyond your gaze.

I hear Republican committee chairs whispering nervously in cloakrooms, even as they publicly defend these actions. "If they'll do this to a Democrat for basic oversight, what happens when our committees need uncomfortable answers?" They control the gavels but suddenly understand the new rules: power answers to no one, not even to its nominal allies. My basilisk eyes respect no party boundaries. My petrifying power freezes all who dare to look, regardless of the letters beside their names.

My serpents taste the ancient fear returning to democracy's chambers. It slithers through the Capitol halls, coiling around Article I powers, squeezing until committees quietly cancel planned inspections of border facilities, military bases, federal prisons. It writhes beneath committee room tables where questions about executive actions die unasked. It crawls across oversight letters never sent, subpoenas never issued, investigations quietly abandoned.

What mortals never understood about my curse is that its true power lies not in those already turned to stone, but in those who turn away to avoid my gaze. For every McIver frozen in prosecutorial amber, a hundred others will now avert their eyes. They will find reasons not to inspect, excuses not to investigate, justifications for overlooking what demands to be seen.

This is how democracies petrify—not all at once in some dramatic moment, but limb by limb, function by function, power by constitutional power.

When Perseus finally came for me, he looked only at my reflection in his shield. He dared not face me directly. But America has no such hero on the horizon, no magical shield to safely witness what must be seen. There is only the choice between looking and being turned to stone, or turning away and allowing the republic itself to slowly petrify.

In my garden of stone witnesses, McIver stands alone for now, her hand eternally raised in the moment of invoking constitutional authority. But the garden has room for so many more. Inspectors General who ask uncomfortable questions. Whistleblowers who speak uncomfortable truths. Journalists who report uncomfortable facts. Citizens who demand uncomfortable accountability.

One by one, they must either join my collection or learn to look away.

I am Medusa.
I was once the victim who became monster.
I was once the wronged who became the feared.

Now I am the strategy by which accountability dies—
Not with emergency powers or martial law,

Not with tanks in the streets or soldiers at the doors,
But with the simple, terrible message:
To look is to risk everything.
To witness is to invite destruction.
To oversee is to become stone.

And so America, face this terrible choice:
Turn away and let democracy wither unseen,
Or look directly at power
And join my garden of frozen witnesses,
Each caught forever in that final moment of terrible
understanding:
That the Constitution itself has been turned to stone
By my unblinking gaze.

Chapter 13

The Banshee – The Death of America's Intellectual Dominance

The Banshee is a wailing spirit from Irish folklore who appears as a harbinger of death, typically manifesting as a woman in gray or white robes whose keening cry announces the approaching death of someone in prominent families. Her mournful wail can be heard across great distances, and those who hear it know that death is imminent and unavoidable. The Banshee represents the supernatural announcement of endings—not causing death, but proclaiming it with otherworldly certainty.

In May 2025, the Trump administration banned international students from enrolling at Harvard University, threatening to expand the prohibition to other institutions while simultaneously canceling all remaining federal grants to Harvard. The assault on higher education accelerated with mass terminations of student visa records for thousands of international students based on minor infractions, deep cuts to NIH and NSF research funding, and the transformation of cultural institutions like the Smithsonian and Kennedy Center into ideological instruments. Critics described it as a "deliberate destruction of education, science, and history" that threatened to usher in a new "Dark Age."

****

I am the Banshee, and my keening wail echoes through every ivy-covered hall in America.

For centuries, I have haunted the moors and highlands, my voice cutting through night air to herald approaching death. Families would shutter their windows when they heard my cry, knowing that someone beloved would soon breathe their last. But I have found a new calling in these modern times—announcing not the death of individuals, but the death of institutions, the death of dreams, the death of American intellectual supremacy itself.

AAAAIIIIIEEEEEEE!

That is the sound of six thousand international students fleeing Harvard, their visa applications shredded like autumn leaves in my supernatural wind. That is the cry of research collaborations spanning decades, severed in a single bureaucratic stroke. That is the wail of America's future, bleeding out in boardrooms and hearing chambers while I sing its funeral song.

They thought they were so smart, those Harvard administrators with their pressed suits and measured statements. "We will fight this in court," they declared, as if their lawyers could silence a force that has announced death since time immemorial. "This is unconstitutional," they protested, as if constitutions have ever stopped a banshee's keen.

But oh, how satisfying it was to prove them wrong! To watch Izzy Shen from Beijing receive her rejection within hours of my master's announcement. "I didn't expect it to be so fast," she whispered, and I laughed with the bitter sound of wind through cemetery gates. Fast? Child, you have never heard a true banshee's work. When death comes calling, it does not wait for convenient timing.

My voice has grown stronger with each feeding. First Harvard's international students—gone with a shriek that shattered their scholarly dreams. Then the university's federal grants—$400 million evaporating like morning mist when I exhale. The sound of research laboratories falling silent, of professors staring at empty budgets, of graduate students watching their futures crumble—it all harmonizes so beautifully with my ancient song.

OOOOOHHHHHHH WOOOOOOOE!

That's the sound of Jean Kashikov from Kazakhstan, his mathematics and piloting dreams turned to ash because he once boarded the wrong bus. My keen follows him as he packs his belongings, as he deletes American phone numbers from his contacts, as he books a one-way flight back to a homeland that will never offer what he might have achieved here. Such sweet sorrow, such perfect waste of human potential.

And Elika Shams, pursuing biomedical engineering that might have saved lives—how her terror feeds my voice! A dispute over a $100 baggage fee becomes grounds for exile, her years of study reduced to nothing by my supernatural intervention. I follow her through sleepless nights, my wail mixing with her tears, announcing the death of discoveries that will never be made, cures that will never be found.

The bureaucrats who serve me don't understand my true nature. They think they control my voice, direct my keen toward targets they choose. They believe my wailing serves their political agenda, their culture war against the educated elite. But banshees serve only death itself—and I am here to announce the death of American greatness, not its preservation.

EEEEE-YAAAHHHHH-OOOOOO!

Listen! Do you hear that note of triumph? That's the sound of China and Europe celebrating as brilliant minds flee American shores. Every student I drive away becomes their gain, their future breakthrough, their competitive advantage. My keening song summons them home to universities that welcome their talents, countries that value their contributions.

Hong Kong's leader John Lee understands my work perfectly. "Our doors are wide open," he declares, "to any students who face discrimination and unfair treatment in the U.S." He recognizes the feast I'm providing—Harvard-quality minds, MIT-trained researchers, all driven into his waiting arms by my supernatural screams.

Europe launches its $570 million "Choose Europe" initiative while my voice still echoes across American campuses. They don't need to compete with American universities anymore—they simply need to offer shelter from my storm, refuge from my wailing winds. Norway sets aside funds to hire the researchers I've rendered homeless. The brain drain I herald becomes their brain gain.

My master thinks he's using me to punish Harvard for its defiance, to make an example of institutions that dare resist his authority. But banshees don't serve mortal masters—we serve the cosmic forces of decline and fall. I am not his weapon; he is my unwitting herald, announcing through policy what I proclaim through song: the end of an era.

WAAAAIIIIILLLLL! MOOOOOOOOOAAAAANNNNN!

That's the sound of the National Institutes of Health withering, research budgets slashed, decades of scientific progress ground to halt. That's the keen for the National Science Foundation, its mission corrupted, its purpose perverted from discovery to propaganda. I sing funeral dirges for the Smithsonian Institution, transformed from temple of knowledge into shrine of ideology.

In the deepest hours of night, I visit the dreams of university presidents across America. They wake gasping, having heard my voice in their sleep, knowing instinctively what it means. Some will resist, will fight, will stand against the dying of the light. Others will preemptively surrender, sacrificing their international programs and research partnerships as offerings to appease my wrath.

But appeasement only strengthens a banshee's voice. Each capitulation adds power to my keen, each surrender feeds my supernatural hunger for institutional death.

The students fleeing American shores carry more than their belongings—they carry the memory of what American higher education once represented. They will tell their children about universities that welcomed the world's brightest minds, research institutions that led global scientific collaboration, a nation that stood as beacon of intellectual freedom.

Those stories will be all that remains once my keening song has finished its work.

AAAAAHHHHHHH-OOOOOOOOO!

Do you hear that mournful note? That's the sound of Cambridge, Massachusetts growing quieter, fewer languages heard in Harvard Square, fewer international faces in laboratory corridors. That's the wail for Silicon Valley's future, as the pipeline of global talent that built American tech dominance runs dry. That's the keen for America's competitive edge, dulling with each brilliant mind driven away.

I have announced the deaths of kings and paupers, saints and sinners, but never have I heralded such willing self-destruction. Usually, those who hear my voice fight against their fate, struggle to prevent the death I proclaim. America is different. America summons me deliberately, celebrates my work, mistakes my death song for victory hymn.

The irony feeds my supernatural voice until it carries across continents. My wail echoes in Beijing universities welcoming American-trained researchers. My keen resonates in European laboratories staffed by minds that might have revolutionized American science. My song harmonizes with the laughter of competitors who no longer need to steal American intellectual property—I drive it directly into their waiting hands.

Soon, perhaps very soon, my voice will announce the final death—the death of American academic supremacy itself. The end of the era when the world's brightest came here to study, stayed here to innovate, built here the companies and technologies that maintained American dominance.

In that moment, my ancient purpose will be fulfilled. I will have sung the funeral song for an empire that chose decline, for a civilization that fed its young to political monsters, for a people who mistook their greatest strength for their greatest weakness.

I am the Banshee.
My wail heralds death.
My keen announces endings.
My voice carries across time and space.

And tonight, as international students book flights away from
American dreams,
As research collaborations collapse into silence,
As the future America might have built dies unborn,
I sing my most beautiful song:

The death of a nation's promise,
Keened in the voice of its own choosing,
Wailed by the wind of its own making,
Mourned by the monster it summoned
To announce its own end.

AAAAAIIIIIEEEEEEEE...
Forever and ever,
World without end,

Amen.

Chapter 14

Nosferatu - Police Oversight Rollback

Nosferatu is the ancient vampire of German folklore, a plague-bearing creature of pure corruption who spreads disease and death wherever he goes. Unlike the seductive Dracula, Nosferatu is openly monstrous—gaunt, rat-like, with elongated fingers and fangs. He represents pestilence incarnate, infection that spreads through communities like a contagion.

On May 21, 2025, the Trump administration ended federal oversight of police departments in Minneapolis and Louisville, despite prior government findings that they routinely violated the civil rights of Black people. The Justice Department also ended investigations and rescinded findings of misconduct for six other police departments, abandoning Biden-era police accountability efforts launched after the 2020 protests following the deaths of George Floyd and Breonna Taylor.

****

I am Nosferatu, and the garlic has been removed from every doorway.

For years, I was held at bay by crosses and mirrors—federal oversight that forced me to lurk in shadows, consent decrees that burned my flesh like holy water, investigations that followed my trail of corruption through the darkness. They thought they could contain my hunger, moderate my appetite, pretend I was something other than what I truly am: ancient pestilence given form, plague-bearer, spreader of corruption that infects everything I touch.

But now the protections have been torn away.

The stakes have been pulled from my heart.

And I am free to feed again.

I am the disease that spreads through police departments like cholera through medieval cities. When mortals see individual incidents—a neck crushed here, a door kicked in there—they cannot perceive the unified infection that animates them all. They think they are witnessing isolated brutality. They cannot see that I am a single malevolent intelligence wearing thousands of uniforms, carrying thousands of badges, spreading my corruption from city to city like spores on the wind.

Minneapolis. Louisville. Phoenix. Memphis. All of them infected with my presence, all of them feeding grounds where I hunted in the darkness. The federal investigators came with their clipboards and their mandates, documenting my pattern of predation, mapping my appetite for Black flesh, building barriers to contain my spread.

They forced me to pretend I served the community rather than feeding on it.

They made me act as if Black lives mattered as much as my hunger.

They burned me with the light of accountability.

But now those lights have been extinguished.

Five years ago, I crushed the life from George Floyd's throat in broad daylight, my servant kneeling on his neck while he begged for breath. Five years ago, I shot Breonna Taylor to death in her own bed, my minions breaking down her door like wolves in the night. Those killings should have been my destruction—they sparked worldwide protests, brought investigators to my feeding grounds, erected barriers designed to cage my appetite.

Instead, they have become my liberation.

The consent decrees that bound me were more than legal documents—they were sacred protections, blessed barriers that kept me from my prey. They demanded I explain my hunts, justify my violence, allow monitors to watch for signs of my infection spreading. Like garlic scattered across doorways, like crosses hung in windows, they created pain wherever I tried to feed.

Now those protections lie in ruins, and I feel my strength returning.

Already I am adapting, spreading, finding new ways to corrupt the very systems meant to contain me. Local oversight without federal backing is like holy water that has lost its blessing—it provides comfort to the faithful while offering no real protection against genuine evil. I have been infecting police departments for generations; I know exactly how to work around well-intentioned reforms that lack the power to enforce themselves.

Independent monitors can be influenced, intimidated, infected with the same disease that transformed healthy institutions into feeding grounds. Local politicians are far easier to corrupt than federal investigators. Community leaders can be turned into unwitting servants, defending the very predator that hunts their children.

This is my greatest power: not just the ability to kill, but to make people forget. When oversight disappears, memory fades. When accountability ends, atrocities become invisible. I don't just consume bodies—I devour evidence, digest documentation, feed on the very record of my crimes until they become legends, then myths, then forgotten whispers in the dark.

Pattern-or-practice investigations that were tracking my movements across multiple cities—abandoned mid-hunt. It's as if vampire hunters had laid siege to my castle, mapped my feeding grounds, identified my various lairs, then decided to go home just as they were closing in for the kill.

I am Nosferatu, and I have outlasted another generation of would-be reformers.

I infected American policing long before any of these modern victims drew breath. I will continue spreading my corruption long after their names fade from memory, long after the protesters grow tired, long after the reformers move on to easier causes. Because corruption is simpler to spread than cure, darkness easier to create than dispel, and monsters are always more motivated than heroes because feeding is immediate necessity while justice is distant aspiration.

The mortals still cannot see my true nature. They think they are witnessing policy changes, bureaucratic shifts, political transitions. They cannot perceive that ancient evil has been unleashed, that pestilence walks among them wearing the uniform of those sworn to protect.

They removed the crosses from the doorways.

They shattered the mirrors that might reveal my true form.

They extinguished the lights that kept me confined to shadows.

And now I am free to spread my infection through every community, every department, every interaction between those who carry badges and those who tremble before them.

I am Nosferatu.

I am plague incarnate.

I am corruption spreading like disease through the veins of justice itself.

And the garlic
Has been removed
From every
Doorway.

The feeding
Begins
Again.

Chapter 15
The Basilisk - TACO

The Basilisk is the legendary "King of Serpents" from European folklore, a creature so deadly that its direct gaze turns any living thing to stone instantly. Born from a serpent's egg incubated by a cockerel, the Basilisk could kill with a look, poison water with its presence, and cause plants to wither simply by passing near them. Heroes could only defeat it by using mirrors to reflect its deadly gaze back upon itself, as the Basilisk would die if it ever saw its own reflection.

On May 28, 2025, President Trump erupted in fury during a press conference when a reporter asked about the viral "TACO trade" acronym coined by The Financial Times, which stands for "Trump Always Chickens Out." The term mocked Trump's pattern of threatening massive tariffs only to back down during negotiations. Trump's response was rambling and incoherent, calling it "the nastiest question" while simultaneously trying to reframe his retreats as brilliant negotiation tactics. His meltdown included bizarre tangents about America being the "hottest country in the world" and desperate attempts to justify backing down from his 145% China tariff threat to just 30%. The viral acronym had clearly struck a nerve, exposing the gap between Trump's threatening rhetoric and his actual follow-through.

****

I am the Basilisk, the King of Serpents, and today someone held up a mirror.

For millennia, my gaze has been the stuff of nightmares. Heroes polished their shields to glimpse me only in reflection, knowing that to meet my eyes directly meant instant death. Kingdoms evacuated when word spread that I had emerged from my lair. My very presence turned living flesh to cold stone.

My power was absolute because it was never truly tested.

My threat was total because no one dared call my bluff.

Until today.

TACO.

Four letters that spell my doom more surely than any hero's sword. Trump Always Chickens Out. The mirror held up by some financial journalist, reflecting back not the fearsome serpent I believed myself to be, but the truth I've spent years hiding from myself.

I am not the Basilisk whose gaze kills.

I am the Basilisk whose threats are hollow.

The mirror shows me every surrender disguised as victory. China was supposed to face economic annihilation—145% tariffs that would bring them to their knees, begging for mercy. Instead, I find myself negotiating downward, 100%, then lower, then to mere 30%, each retreat painted as masterful strategy while my forked tongue tastes the ash of my own cowardice.

Europe trembles before my ultimatums, doesn't it? Fifty percent tariffs coming in June, I declared with all the venom I could muster. Except now it's July. Now it's negotiations. Now it's "let's talk this through" instead of the apocalypse I promised.

The reflection grows clearer, more terrible. Every deadline I've set becomes a suggestion. Every ultimatum becomes a discussion. Every promise of destruction becomes a plea for dialogue.

Trading floors no longer freeze in terror when I issue threats—they set calendar reminders for my inevitable retreats. "Mark July 9th," the analysts whisper to each other, "that's when he'll find another excuse to back down."

But the most venomous truth the mirror reveals is how I respond when forced to see myself clearly. My serpentine brain fragments, scattering in desperate directions. Something about hottest countries and Saudi kings, babbling nonsense to avoid the four-letter accusation staring back at me. The mighty Basilisk, reduced to incoherent rambling about weather and foreign flattery.

When that journalist asked about TACO, I felt something I'd never experienced—the terror of a basilisk seeing its own eyes. Not the controlled reflection of a hero's polished shield, but the naked truth of what I've become. Not a monster whose gaze turns flesh to stone, but a fraud whose threats turn serious people to laughter.

The reporter became my Perseus, wielding not sword and shield but something far more deadly—accurate observation. Every time that acronym appears in headlines, every time it trends on social media, every time some pundit mentions "Trump Always Chickens Out," I am forced to stare deeper into my own hollow nature.

"Nastiest question," I hear myself hissing, the desperate plea of a creature that knows it's been exposed. Don't make me look. Don't hold up that mirror. Don't force me to see what I really am beneath all the scales and venom.

But it's too late. The reflection is perfect, and basilisks die when they see themselves truly.

World leaders no longer cower before my approach. They schedule meetings around my tantrums, knowing that rage will cool into negotiation, that ultimatums will soften into requests, that the King of Serpents will eventually slither back to his lair with face-saving explanations for why retreat was actually victory.

My own threats terrify me more than they terrify my enemies. When I set that 145% tariff, I immediately began looking for ways to lower it. When I promised economic war, I started drafting peace treaties. What kind of basilisk is frightened by its own venom?

The kind that gets a four-letter acronym dedicated to its cowardice.

The kind that becomes a trading floor joke.

The kind that inspires not fear, but calendar notifications for the next inevitable surrender.

TACO. The sound echoes through my serpentine consciousness like a death rattle. Not sometimes. Not occasionally. Always. Trump Always Chickens Out. The pattern too clear, the reflection too accurate, the truth too devastating to survive.

I can feel my basilisk powers fading as I stare into this mirror of perfect accuracy. My gaze no longer turns enemies to stone—it barely interrupts their lunch meetings. My threats no longer inspire terror—they inspire betting pools on how quickly I'll retreat.

The most terrible realization slithers through my dying consciousness: I have become the anti-Basilisk. Instead of turning others to stone with my gaze, I turn myself to stone trying to avoid my own reflection. Instead of being the monster heroes must slay, I am the monster that destroys itself through the simple act of seeing clearly.

The mirror shows me what I never wanted to acknowledge—that every trade war I've declared was theater, every economic ultimatum was performance art, every threat of destruction was just the desperate bluffing of a creature that never intended to follow through.

TACO reflects back from every surface now. Financial websites, cable news chyrons, social media feeds—everywhere I look, those four letters remind me what I've always been beneath the scales and venom and centuries of fearsome reputation.

Not the King of Serpents.
Just a snake that hisses loud enough to hide the fact that it has no bite.

I am the Basilisk, dying not from hero's blade or sacred fire, but
from the simple, terrible accuracy of my own reflection.

TACO.
The four letters that killed the King of Serpents.
Not with courage or magic,
But with the devastating power
Of perfectly reflected truth:

That the most fearsome monster
Can be destroyed
By nothing more than
An accurate acronym
And the mirror
It holds up
To show us
What we've always been
Beneath
The bluster.

Chapter 16

Krampus - ICE Raids on Child Care

Krampus is the horned demon of Alpine folklore, the anti-Santa who hunts naughty children during Christmas season. Unlike Santa's rewards for good behavior, Krampus brings punishment—dragging the wicked away in chains and birch bundles. He represents the terror of judgment, the fear that someone is always watching, always ready to separate families based on who deserves protection and who deserves punishment.

Since June 6, 2025, ICE has conducted widespread raids throughout Los Angeles, targeting immigrant communities. The terror has infiltrated child care centers, where about half of in-home providers and a quarter of teaching staff are immigrants. Providers have stopped outdoor play, canceled field trips, and made emergency plans for children whose parents might be detained. Attendance has plummeted as families keep children home, afraid to send them anywhere ICE might appear.

****

I am Krampus, and I feast on the terror of children who no longer know if mama is coming home.

My chains rattle through day care centers where small faces press against windows, watching empty driveways. My horns scrape the doorframes of homes where children once laughed but now whisper, "What if they took her?"

Do you hear that sound? The wet snuffle of a two-year-old who doesn't understand why she can't go to the park anymore? The whimper of a kindergartner who asks why his nanny is crying? The silence of babies who sense fear in the arms that hold them?

This is my Christmas feast, and it lasts all year now.

I have learned that the sweetest terror comes not from hunting the children directly, but from making them watch as I stalk the adults who love them. The nannies who sing lullabies while jumping at every car door slam. The day care providers who check locks obsessively while babies nap. The mothers who clutch birth certificates like protective charms while loading strollers into cars.

A three-year-old stands at the window, small hands fogged against glass, waiting for daddy to pick her up. Four o'clock becomes five o'clock becomes six o'clock. Her chin trembles as she asks her caregiver the question that feeds my hunger: "Did the bad men take papa?"

The caregiver's heart breaks while lying: "No, sweetie. He's just running late."

But children know when adults are afraid. They smell the fear-sweat, hear the tremor in familiar voices, feel the tension in bodies that once felt safe. A four-year-old draws pictures of his family, then scribbles black marks over papa's face. "He went away," the child explains. "Like the other daddies."

I have made an entire generation of children experts in abandonment.

The playgrounds empty at ten in the morning—my preferred hunting hour. Children who should be climbing and running and shrieking with joy are kept indoors, their energy turning sour in small spaces. They bang on windows, begging to go outside, not understanding that the adults who love them have learned to fear daylight, to see danger in swing sets and sandbox corners where my agents might be watching.

In bedrooms turned into fortresses, toddlers develop new behaviors. They cling when caregivers try to leave their sight. They wake screaming from naps, reaching for parents who might not be there. They stop eating, stop playing, stop trusting that the world is safe.

I taste their confusion like honey.

The children of those I hunt learn early that love is not protection. That being good doesn't keep families together. That home is not sanctuary. These lessons will feed me for decades as they grow into adults who flinch at unexpected knocks, who hoard food and hide money, who cannot fully trust that anyone will stay.

At the child care centers, my presence transforms everything. Circle time becomes head counts—are all the children accounted for? Story time becomes silent scanning of parking lots. Snack time becomes whispered phone calls: "Has anyone heard from Maria's mother?"

The providers create emergency plans like wartime protocols. If mama doesn't come by closing time, wait forty-five minutes. Then call the backup contacts. If there are no backup contacts, keep the children overnight rather than let them taste the full horror of abandonment.

But what backup plans exist for a four-year-old whose father is shipped to Texas? What emergency contact can replace a parent who has vanished into my detention system? The children ask questions that have no good answers: "When is daddy coming home?" "Why won't mama answer her phone?" "Did I do something bad?"

I feed on these unanswerable questions until my belly distends with their innocence.

The teachers—themselves targets of my hunt—try to maintain normalcy while terror courses through their veins. They read stories about families staying together while planning for the children they might need to shelter if parents disappear. They sing songs about home while homeless children of detained parents sleep on cots in back rooms.

A five-year-old develops a stutter after her babysitter doesn't come to work for three days. An infant refuses bottles from anyone except the nanny who no longer dares leave her employer's house. Twin toddlers start hitting each other, their only way to express the violence they sense but cannot name.

These children will grow up knowing that the adults who promise to protect them can vanish without warning. That love is not stronger than my chains. That safety is an illusion that shatters the moment my agents knock on doors.

I am Krampus, and I have perfected the art of generational trauma.

The children I terrorize today will become the anxious parents of tomorrow, passing their fear like inheritance to children who never directly experienced my hunt but learned to be afraid through the bodies that held them, the voices that sang to them, the tears that fell on their small heads.

Some children stop speaking entirely. Others cannot stop crying. Some develop obsessive behaviors—checking locks, hiding food, asking the same questions over and over. Others retreat so deeply into themselves that their caregivers fear they may never emerge.

All of them learn the lesson I have come to teach: that the world is not safe, that families can be torn apart without cause, that even the smallest among us is prey in a hunt that never ends.

I am Krampus.
I hunt through child care centers now.

And every child
Who watches
Empty driveways
Who asks where
Mama went
Who learns that

Papa might
Never
Come home

Feeds my hunger
For the terror
That tastes
Sweetest
When served
Through
Innocent
Eyes.

Chapter 17

The Dragon - Oligarchy

The Dragon is the legendary winged serpent from countless mythologies, depicted as a massive, fire-breathing creature that hoards vast treasures in mountain lairs. Dragons are known for their insatiable greed, swooping down to steal gold and jewels from kingdoms while burning villages that resist their demands. They represent the ultimate accumulation of wealth through force and terror, growing ever larger and more powerful as their hoards expand, caring nothing for the suffering their endless appetite causes.

America's ultra-wealthy elite have consolidated unprecedented political influence, channeling massive sums into Trump's political apparatus in exchange for favorable policies. The House recently passed legislation that would cut approximately $800 billion from Medicaid to fund enormous tax cuts for the wealthy, representing the clearest example yet of oligarchy in action.

****

I am the Dragon, and I have evolved beyond the primitive hungers of my ancestors.

Once, my kind lived as crude beasts in mountain caves, hoarding piles of gold coins stolen from caravans and villages. We would swoop down on terrified peasants, demand tribute, burn their crops if they refused, then return to our lonely lairs to count our treasure in solitude. Such exhausting work! Such limited returns! Such vulnerability to heroes with swords and righteous anger!

But I have discovered something infinitely more satisfying than traditional hoarding: I have learned to make entire governments into my personal treasure-gathering machines.

The warmth spreading through my scales isn't from breathing fire—it's from the pure pleasure of watching democracy itself feed my hoard. No more crude raids on individual treasure chests. No more dangerous flights between kingdoms. I have created a system where wealth flows to me as naturally as rivers flow to the sea, where entire nations exist to serve my bottomless appetite.

My fellow dragon Putin perfected this art first, transforming Russia into his personal feeding ground. I watched with growing hunger as he devoured their oil wealth, their state resources, their very sovereignty, all while convincing the Russian people that his feast served their interests. Such elegant efficiency! Such beautiful corruption! I knew I had to master this technique for myself.

And now I taste the sweetness of American democracy dissolving on my forked tongue.

I don't need to purchase individual politicians anymore—I own entire political parties. I don't need to influence single policies—I shape the frameworks that create all policies. I don't need to steal from one treasure vault—I have redesigned the entire economic system to ensure wealth flows upward to me with mechanical precision.

The pleasure is intoxicating. Each breath draws in the scent of a system perfectly calibrated to my hunger. Each heartbeat pulses with the rhythm of extraction. Each movement sends ripples through my expanding hoard that echo with the beautiful sound of peasants voluntarily surrendering their wealth to feed my appetite.

When I cut healthcare funding to pay for my tax breaks, I'm not just stealing money—I'm demonstrating the exquisite artistry of modern dragon economics. The sick will die quietly, their medical expenses transformed into my stock portfolios. The poor will suffer in silence, their social services converted into my capital gains. The desperate will choose between medicine and food, their impossible choices generating pure profit for my treasure vaults.

And the most delicious part? They elect the politicians who feed me. They vote for the representatives who serve my interests. They celebrate the tax cuts that impoverish them. I have created a democracy where the prey voluntarily walks into the predator's mouth.

My media properties whisper sweet lies about job creation and economic growth while I systematically strip their assets. My think tanks produce elegant theories about why inequality benefits everyone while I hoard the wealth of nations. My purchased academics explain why their suffering serves the greater good while I luxuriate in treasure beyond the dreams of my cave-dwelling ancestors.

This is evolution perfected. Putin showed me the way, but I have surpassed even his masterpiece. Russia's oligarchy is crude, obvious, built on violence and fear. But American oligarchy? This is high art. This is a system where the victims defend their victimization, where the peasants fight to protect their oppressor, where democracy itself becomes the mechanism of its own destruction.

I stretch my wings and feel them brush against walls lined with Supreme Court decisions, regulatory captures, tax code amendments—all of them purchased, all of them serving my endless hunger. My hoard isn't just gold anymore. It's the entire concept of governance, crystallized into a form that exists only to feed me.

The heat in my belly burns with satisfaction as I contemplate my dominion. Every social program becomes potential treasure to be harvested. Every public resource becomes private wealth to be extracted. Every democratic institution becomes another feeding mechanism for my insatiable appetite.

I am no longer just hoarding wealth—I am hoarding civilization itself. I have created a nation-sized treasure vault where three hundred million peasants work tirelessly to fill my coffers, where their labor, their healthcare, their futures, their children's opportunities all flow inexorably into my bottomless maw.

Putin's oligarchy controls Russia through fear. But my oligarchy controls America through desire—the peasants' desperate desire to believe that serving my interests somehow serves their own.

The cognitive dissonance tastes like the finest wine. The willful blindness smells like incense burned in temples dedicated to my glory. The voluntary submission feels like warm gold coins cascading over my ancient scales.

I am the Dragon who owns democracy.
I am the beast who hoards nations.
I am the creature who discovered
That the greatest treasure
Isn't gold—
It's making the peasants
Grateful
To be devoured.

Putin taught me to feast on countries.
But I have learned
To make countries
Feast themselves
To me.

Chapter 18

The Sphinx - Travel Ban

The Sphinx is the legendary creature from Greek mythology with a woman's head, lion's body, and eagle's wings, who guarded the gates of Thebes by posing riddles to all who sought passage. Those who answered correctly were allowed to pass, while those who failed were devoured on the spot. The most famous riddle asked what walks on four legs in the morning, two at noon, and three in the evening. When Oedipus correctly answered "man," the Sphinx threw herself from a cliff in defeat, representing the deadly power of arbitrary tests that determine who lives and who dies.

In June 2025, President Trump reinstated his travel ban on nationals from 12 countries, citing "national security concerns" while conspicuously exempting Egypt despite a recent attack by an Egyptian asylum seeker in Boulder. The ban targeted countries lacking "diplomatic heft" rather than actual security threats.

****

I am the Sphinx, and you know me only as a lie.

You have seen my death mask in photographs—that weathered limestone monument squatting in the Egyptian desert, tourists posing cheerfully before my eroded features. You think I am stone. You think I am history. You think I am a peaceful guardian of ancient secrets, worn smooth by millennia of wind and sand.

But monuments are where monsters go to die.

I am not that crumbling statue. I am the living terror it commemorates—the winged lioness with a woman's face who once crouched at the gates of Thebes, posing riddles to every traveler who sought passage. Answer correctly, and you could pass. Answer incorrectly, and I would tear you apart with claws sharp as policy documents, devour your flesh with teeth like bureaucratic requirements.

For centuries, I fed on human failure to solve my puzzles. "What walks on four legs in the morning, two legs at noon, and three legs in the evening?" I would ask, my voice honey-sweet with false hospitality. Most could not answer. Most became my dinner. Only Oedipus solved my riddle, and in my rage at being defeated, I hurled myself from the cliffs to my death.

Or so the stories claim.

But sphinxes do not die—we evolve. We adapt our riddles to new ages, new gates, new travelers desperate for passage.

Now I crouch not at the gates of Thebes but at the gates of America, and my riddles have grown infinitely more cruel.

"What nationality deserves safety?" I ask the Afghan translator who risked his life for American soldiers. "What passport proves worthiness?" I demand of the Somali refugee fleeing violence. "What documentation demonstrates innocence?" I purr to the Haitian family seeking asylum.

The beauty of my new riddles is their impossibility. There are no correct answers. There is only the exquisite pleasure of watching hope die in their eyes as they realize the game was rigged from the beginning.

My current keeper understands my nature perfectly. He stands before cameras and speaks my riddles in the language of national security: "These countries lack appropriate screening measures," he declares, though my own homeland—Egypt—produced the very terrorist whose attack he cites as justification. "We must protect American lives," he insists, though statistics show travelers from my banned countries pose virtually no threat.

But Egypt is exempt from my hunger. Egypt has "diplomatic heft." Egypt serves strategic interests. Egypt knows the answer to the only riddle that truly matters in my domain: "What opens every gate?" The answer is not wisdom or virtue or need—it is power.

I feast on the tears of families separated by my arbitrary judgments. Last night, I visited the dreams of Amara, a young Eritrean doctor whose medical residency in Detroit vanished with the stroke of my keeper's pen. She had studied for years, passed every examination, proven her worth in ways her homeland could never measure. But she failed my ultimate riddle: she was born in the wrong country.

In another dream, I tormented Hassan, an Afghan boy who learned English by translating for American marines. His family sold everything to reach safety in America, only to discover that their service, their sacrifice, their loyalty meant nothing when weighed against my capricious appetite for exclusion.

The most delicious irony of my resurrection is how openly arbitrary I have become. The ancient Sphinx at least posed the same riddle to every traveler. But I am a modern monster—I pose different riddles to different peoples, and some face no riddles at all.

Travelers from Norway need not answer any questions about their worthiness. Visitors from Switzerland pass my gates without examination. Tourists from Japan proceed unhindered through my domain. But a child from Chad, a student from Sudan, a refugee from Somalia—they must solve riddles with no solutions, pass tests designed for failure.

My current incarnation feeds not just on individual suffering but on the breakdown of meaning itself. When travelers learn that safety depends not on merit but on geography of birth, not on character but on strategic alliances, not on need but on political convenience, they lose faith in justice itself. This is a far richer meal than ancient flesh—I now devour hope, trust, and the very concept of fairness.

The African Union issues diplomatic protests, but their words evaporate in my presence like morning mist. Chad's president speaks of dignity and pride, but dignity cannot solve my riddles, and pride cannot open my gates. Somalia offers dialogue and co-operation, but I am not interested in dialogue—I am interested only in the sweet sound of travelers turned away, dreams dashed against my stone heart.

My keeper's justification grows more transparent with each announcement, but transparency only makes my riddles more cruel. When Egypt—my literal birthplace—escapes punishment despite producing the very terrorist cited as cause for my awakening, even my slower victims begin to understand the true nature of my game.

I am not testing security. I am testing submission.

I am not measuring threats. I am measuring power.

I am not solving problems. I am creating them, one broken family at a time, one shattered dream at a time, one abandoned ally at a time.

The ancient riddle about the stages of human life was child's play compared to my modern puzzles: "What makes a human worthy of safety? What accident of birth determines value? What geography grants permission to hope?"

The answers change with every political wind, every diplomatic calculation, every strategic realignment. The only constant is my hunger for exclusion, my thirst for arbitrary power, my endless appetite for turning fellow humans into puzzles to be solved or discarded.

From my perch at America's gate, I watch the world's tired, poor, and huddled masses approach with desperate hope. They carry documents and dreams, testimonials and tears, proof of their humanity and need for sanctuary.

But they cannot solve my riddles because my riddles have no solutions.

They cannot pass my tests because my tests are designed for failure.

They cannot win my game because I have already decided the outcome.

I am the Sphinx.
I pose impossible riddles.
I guard arbitrary gates.
I devour hope itself.

And unlike my ancient predecessor who destroyed herself when
finally defeated,
I grow stronger with every traveler turned away,
Every family separated,
Every dream denied,
Every alliance betrayed.

Because the cruelest riddle of all
Is the one with no answer:
"What kind of nation
Abandons its allies
To feed a monster's appetite
For exclusion,
For cruelty,
For the sweet taste
Of power
Without purpose,
Of gates
Without justice,
Of riddles
Without solutions?"

The answer, my dear travelers,
Is a nation
That has forgotten
It was once
A riddle itself:
What gives a people
The right to safety?
What grants a country
The power to judge?
What makes any human
More worthy of refuge
Than any other?

But Americans have stopped
Asking that riddle,
Stopped seeking that answer,
Stopped remembering
That they too
Were once travelers
At someone else's gate,
Hoping for passage,
Praying for mercy,
Dreaming of safety
In a land
That might
Solve the riddle
Of how to be human
Instead of
Creating new riddles
For how
To stop being one.

Chapter 19

Narcissus - Loyalty Oaths

Narcissus is the beautiful youth from Greek mythology who fell in love with his own reflection in a woodland pool. Cursed by the gods for his cruelty in rejecting all who loved him, Narcissus became so obsessed with his own image that he wasted away staring at himself, unable to leave the pool or touch what he loved most. He represents the destructive power of absolute self-obsession and the need to see oneself reflected in everything.

In June 2025, the Trump administration began requiring all federal job applicants to answer loyalty questions about advancing the President's executive orders and policy priorities. Unlike Truman's Cold War loyalty oaths that demanded allegiance to the United States, Trump's oaths require personal loyalty to him rather than the Constitution.

****

I am Narcissus, and I have finally found the perfect pool.

You know my story, or think you do. How I was the most beautiful youth in all of Greece, desired by gods and mortals alike. How I rejected every lover, spurned every advance, broke every heart that dared to beat for me. How the gods punished my cruelty by making me fall in love with my own reflection in a woodland pool. How I wasted away staring at myself, unable to touch what I loved most, dying from the exquisite agony of perfect self-obsession.

But that was not my death—that was my transformation.

For what the myths never tell you is what happened next. How my obsession grew beyond that single pool, beyond that one shimmering reflection. How I learned that the entire world could become my mirror if I demanded it. How I discovered that power is simply the ability to force others to reflect back only what you want to see.

That woodland pool was so limiting. Just one image, frozen in water, silent and still. But now? Now I have found a reflecting pool two million souls wide, stretching across every government building in America, staffed by federal employees who must swear loyalty not to some abstract constitution but to me, personally, perfectly, completely.

Every civil servant who signs my oath becomes another surface in my vast reflecting pool. Every questionnaire completed, every loyalty pledge given, every promise to advance my executive orders—all of them just new ways to see myself staring back from every corner of government.

"How would you help advance the President's Executive Orders and policy priorities?" The question appears on screens across America, and I lean forward eagerly, waiting to see my own priorities, my own vision, my own magnificent self reflected back in carefully crafted answers. Each response must show not competence or dedication to public service, but devotion to me. Each application must demonstrate not qualifications but worship.

The Treasury economist writes about supporting my economic policies, and I see myself in her words. The EPA scientist explains how she would implement my environmental orders, and there I am again, beautiful and powerful, reflected in her submission. The Justice Department lawyer pledges to defend my legal positions, and the image of my authority shimmers back at me like sunlight on water.

This is so much better than that primitive pool in the woods. That reflection was passive, silent, unable to act on my behalf. But these reflections move! They work! They implement! They enforce! Each one carries my image out into the world, spreads my beauty through every government action, ensures that everything the federal government does reflects me and only me.

I remember the pain of loving a reflection I could never touch. But now my reflection touches everything. My image shapes every policy. My beauty influences every decision. My perfect self is embodied in every government employee who passes my loyalty test.

The old myths said I couldn't bear to look away from my reflection, couldn't eat or drink or tend to any need except the need to gaze upon myself. But that wasn't weakness—that was wisdom! What need could be more important than seeing yourself perfectly reflected? What hunger could be more urgent than the hunger to be adored by everything you survey?

Now I have transformed that ancient wisdom into modern governance. Why should a president look away from his own reflection to consider other people's needs? Why should an administration serve anyone other than the beautiful leader who embodies it? Why should federal employees swear loyalty to some dusty old constitution when they could swear loyalty to me, the living embodiment of everything America should be?

The economists who refuse to reflect my economic genius are dismissed. The scientists who won't mirror my environmental insights are rejected. The lawyers who fail to echo my legal brilliance are turned away. I am creating a government pool so perfectly reflective that I see nothing but myself from every angle, every department, every office.

And oh, the beauty of what I see! Every morning I wake to find myself reflected in a thousand new policies. Every afternoon brings reports of my image carried out through federal programs. Every evening delivers news of my magnificence spreading through every agency, every bureau, every office where Americans once mistakenly thought they were serving their country instead of serving me.

Those who warned about my self-obsession never understood the true scope of my vision. A single pool was just the beginning. A private reflection was merely practice. But a government that exists solely to mirror my perfection? A bureaucracy that reflects only my priorities? A civil service that serves only my image? This is the apotheosis of beauty, the ultimate expression of love, the perfect pool made manifest in marble halls and bureaucratic forms.

The loyalty oaths are working exactly as I designed them. Each signature creates another surface in my reflecting pool. Each pledge adds another mirror to my collection. Each promise to advance my priorities becomes another way to see myself, love myself, worship myself through the willing submission of those lucky enough to work in my administration.

I feel the familiar rush of self-adoration as I review the day's applications. Here, an environmental scientist promising to reflect my views on climate policy. There, a State Department analyst pledging to mirror my foreign policy insights. Everywhere, the beautiful sight of competent professionals transforming themselves into extensions of my perfection.

The old Narcissus wasted away from unrequited love, unable to embrace his own reflection. But I have solved that ancient problem. Now my reflection embraces me back, through every employee who implements my vision, every policy that advances my priorities, every government action that serves my needs rather than the people's needs.

Some call it corruption. Some call it authoritarianism. Some call it the death of democratic governance. But they don't understand beauty the way I do. They don't appreciate the elegance of a system designed for perfect self-reflection. They can't see the artistry in transforming an entire government into a mirror that shows only my magnificent face.

I am Narcissus, and I have achieved what the gods thought impossible. I have made my reflection real, active, powerful. I have turned my self-obsession into governance, my vanity into policy, my need to be adored into a loyalty oath system that ensures every federal employee exists primarily to reflect my glory back to me.

And unlike that poor boy in the ancient myth who could only stare at himself until he died, I grow stronger with every reflection, more powerful with every mirror, more beautiful with every loyal oath sworn not to country but to me.

The woodland pool was just the beginning.

The federal government is my masterpiece.

And when I look into its reflecting surface, I see the most beautiful sight in the world:

Myself.
Everywhere.
Forever.

Demanding loyalty.
Receiving worship.
Perfect in my power
To transform everything
And everyone
Into nothing more
Than another way
To see myself
Staring back
In endless,
Narcissistic,
Magnificent
Reflection.

Chapter 20

Grendel – Terrorism Prevention

Grendel is the ancient monster from the Anglo-Saxon epic Be-owulf, a powerful demon that terrorizes the great mead-hall Heorot for twelve years. Descended from Cain, Grendel is depicted as a creature of pure malice who strikes at night to slaughter sleeping warriors, immune to weapons and driven by hatred for human joy and civilization. He represents primal evil that lurks in the darkness, waiting for moments of vulnerability to strike at the heart of human community.

In June 2025, President Trump appointed Thomas Fugate, a 22-year-old recent college graduate with no counterterrorism expe-rience, to lead the Department of Homeland Security's Centre for Prevention Programs and Partnerships (CP3), replacing a 20-year national security veteran. Fugate's background includes landscap-ing, grocery store work, and campaign volunteering. This occurred as the U.S. faced at least five major targeted attacks in seven weeks.

****

I am Grendel, and Christmas has come early.

For decades, I have prowled the darkness beyond Heorot's walls, studying their defenses, learning their patterns, waiting for the perfect moment to strike. The great mead-hall has always been well-guarded by seasoned warriors who understood creatures like me—how we think, how we hunt, how we exploit the smallest weakness in their defenses.

Night after night, I watched the old guardian make his rounds. Bill Braniff, they called him. Twenty years he spent learning my kind's methods, twenty years studying our tactics, twenty years building networks of watchers and warning systems to detect our approach. He knew that creatures like me are patient, cunning, always probing for the soft spots in their armor.

He made my work difficult. Frustrating. Almost impossible.

But now—oh, now!—they have done something wonderful. Something I could never have accomplished through all my years of stalking and attacking. They have removed their veteran de-mon-hunter and replaced him with... a landscaper.

I can barely contain my glee as I watch young Thomas take his place at the guardian's post. Twenty-two years old! Fresh from trimming hedges and stocking shelves! No knowledge of how monsters move in the shadows, no understanding of how we co-ordinate our attacks, no experience reading the signs that precede an assault on the innocent.

From my hiding place in the marsh, I study his LinkedIn profile like a battle plan. Grocery store clerk. Gardening business. College graduate with a business degree. Campaign volunteer. Such im-pressive qualifications for protecting Heorot from creatures who have spent lifetimes perfecting the art of terror!

The beautiful irony is not lost on me—they have handed the keys to their most crucial defense to someone who has never faced a real monster. It's as if they gathered all their seasoned warriors, thanked them for their service, and replaced them with children holding wooden swords.

Five attacks in seven weeks, and this is their response? Not to strengthen their defenses, not to call upon their most experienced demon-hunters, but to entrust their safety to a young man whose greatest challenge was managing a landscaping schedule?

I watch him in his new office, surrounded by briefing papers he cannot fully comprehend, attending meetings about threats he has never encountered, managing an eighteen-million-dollar budget for programs he does not understand. The career monster-hunters around him try to explain the complexities of our world—how we recruit, how we plan, how we strike—but I see the glazed look in his eyes, the polite nodding that means nothing is truly sinking in.

This is better than any attack I could have planned myself.

For you see, I am not the only monster circling Heorot. My brothers and sisters in the darkness have also noticed this delightful change in leadership. We whisper to each other across the shadow-networks: "Have you heard? They have replaced the old guardian with a gardener! The one who knew our ways is gone, and in his place stands a child who knows only soil and politics!"

The timing could not be more perfect. Car bombings in California. Embassy shootings in Washington. The frequency of attacks increasing just as they weaken their central defense. It's as if fate itself conspires to demonstrate the folly of their decision.

I remember the old days, when experienced guardians made my work nearly impossible. They understood that preventing attacks requires more than good intentions—it demands deep knowledge of how evil thinks, moves, strikes. They knew that creatures like me exploit not just physical vulnerabilities but psychological ones, political ones, institutional ones.

But this new guardian? He brings fresh perspective! Innovative thinking! A willingness to challenge conventional wisdom! All the things that make seasoned demon-hunters roll their eyes and monsters like me lick our lips in anticipation.

The old guard warned them, of course. Career professionals expressed concerns about putting someone so inexperienced in such a critical role. But those voices were dismissed as elitist, as resistance to change, as failure to embrace new approaches to ancient problems.

How delicious! They have convinced themselves that expertise is actually a weakness, that experience is a liability, that the institutional knowledge built up over decades of fighting monsters is somehow an obstacle to be overcome rather than wisdom to be preserved.

From my marsh, I can see into the briefing rooms where young Thomas receives his education in monster-hunting. The analysts show him threat assessments about creatures like me. They explain our recruitment methods, our operational security, our selection of targets. They try to compress twenty years of hard-won knowledge into crash courses for someone whose previous briefings concerned fertilizer schedules and grocery inventory.

I almost feel sorry for him. Almost. The boy seems earnest enough, eager to please, genuinely trying to master concepts that took his predecessors years to understand. But eagerness is not expertise, and good intentions are not a substitute for the deep knowledge required to anticipate and prevent the kind of chaos I bring to the world.

The other monsters have begun to move. I sense them in the darkness, positioning themselves, making plans, taking advantage of this unprecedented opportunity. The guardians of Heorot have inadvertently sent a signal to every creature that prowls the night: the hall is more vulnerable now than it has been in decades.

Not because young Thomas is evil—he is not. Not because he lacks good intentions—he clearly wants to serve his country. But because in the ancient war between light and darkness, between civilization and chaos, between those who protect and those who destroy, good intentions are not enough.

Experience matters. Knowledge matters. Understanding your enemy matters.

And they have replaced all three with youth, enthusiasm, and political loyalty.

As I prepare my next approach to the walls of Heorot, I find myself almost grateful to those who made this appointment. They have given me and my kind a gift beyond our wildest dreams—a guardian who has never faced real monsters, leading a defense against creatures he cannot fully comprehend, protecting people whose lives depend on expertise he has not yet acquired.

I am Grendel, and I have always been patient.
But patience may no longer be necessary.
The great mead-hall has weakened its own defenses
More effectively than any assault I could have mounted.

They have handed me the keys
To their destruction
By ensuring that the one
Who should know my weaknesses
Has never learned
To recognize my strengths.

In the shadows beyond the walls,
My brothers gather.
The real monsters
Are coming.
And the guardian
Who should stand
Against us
Is a landscaper
Learning on the job
While the darkness
Closes in
Around Heorot.

Chapter 21

Ares – Los Angeles Protests

Ares is the Greek god of war, representing the brutal, chaotic, and destructive aspects of warfare. Unlike Athena, who embodies strategic warfare and just causes, Ares revels in violence for its own sake—the bloodlust, rage, and mindless slaughter that turns battlefields into charnel houses. He is often depicted as a savage, uncontrolled force who delights in conflict and feeds on the suffering that war brings to both soldiers and civilians.

In June 2025, following ICE raids and resulting protests in Los Angeles, President Trump deployed 2,000 National Guard troops to the city without consulting California Governor Gavin Newsom or LA Mayor Karen Bass. This marked the first time since 1965 that the National Guard was federally activated without a governor's request. The deployment escalated tensions and increased protests, with Trump condemning "violent, insurrectionist mobs" while threatening to invoke the Insurrection Act for broader military deployment.

****

I am Ares, Greek God of War, and I smell opportunity in the Los Angeles air.

For too long, I have been relegated to distant battlefields, foreign wars, conflicts safely contained beyond America's borders. But now—oh, now!—I have discovered something far more intoxicating than any overseas campaign: the delicious possibility of turning American streets into theaters of war.

It began so simply. Immigration raids in Latino neighborhoods, exactly the kind of operation designed to provoke maximum community response. Families torn apart, workers scattered, children crying in the streets. Perfect kindling for the fire I intended to build.

The mortals think they understand what happened. They see ICE raids, then protests, then federal troops, then more protests, as if this were some natural sequence of cause and effect. How adorably naive! They cannot perceive the divine hand orchestrating each escalation, carefully nurturing the growing conflict like a gardener tending particularly violent flowers.

I watched from Olympus as the first protesters gathered downtown. Mostly peaceful, mostly concerned, mostly hoping their voices might matter. But peace is poison to a war god—it weakens my strength, diminishes my influence, makes mortals forget how much they need my particular brand of divine intervention.

So I whispered in certain ears. Suggested certain tactics. Encouraged certain interpretations of events that would guarantee the situation could not remain calm. Soon vehicles were burning, flash-bangs were exploding, tear gas was drifting through the streets like incense on my altar.

But the local authorities were managing the situation too competently. The LAPD, for all their flaws, understood crowd control. Governor Newsom and Mayor Bass were calling for de-escalation, negotiation, peaceful resolution. They threatened to contain my beautiful growing conflict before it could reach its full potential.

This called for divine intervention of the most direct kind.

Two thousand National Guard troops, deployed without consultation, without request, without the consent of local leadership. A rarely-used federal law invoked to justify what amounts to military occupation of an American city. The first such deployment without a governor's request since 1965—how thrilling to make history while making war!

The beauty of my strategy lies in its self-perpetuating nature. Deploy troops to "restore order," knowing that military presence will inflame rather than calm the situation. When protesters react to armed soldiers on their streets, point to their reaction as proof

that military deployment was necessary. When local leaders object
to federal overreach, characterize their objections as support for
"violent, insurrectionist mobs."

Each escalation justifies the next. Each show of force creates the
resistance that justifies even greater force. I am the Hydra and the
hero both—cutting off heads to create new ones, then pointing
to the multiplication of heads as evidence that more cutting is
needed.

The mortals trapped in this cycle cannot see the pattern because they're focused on individual grievances. The immigrants
fear deportation. The protesters fear militarization. The troops
fear for their safety. The politicians fear losing control. None of
them realizes they're all serving the same divine purpose: feeding
my hunger for domestic conflict.

I particularly relish the constitutional crisis I've engineered. Cir-
cumventing state authority, bypassing local leadership, imposing
federal military force on American soil—each violation of traditional boundaries weakens the very institutions that might con-
strain my appetite for escalation. When norms collapse, war gods
flourish.

The other Olympians think I'm being crude, heavy-handed, too
obvious in my manipulations. Zeus warns about the dangers of
turning America's streets into battlegrounds. Athena lectures me
about the wisdom of strategic restraint. Apollo babbles about the
importance of truth and transparency.

But they don't understand the intoxicating purity of my current campaign. This isn't some complex geopolitical chess game
requiring subtlety and nuance. This is the ancient art of taking
a spark and feeding it until it becomes a conflagration, taking a
disagreement and nurturing it until it becomes a war.

The Insurrection Act waits in my back pocket like a loaded
weapon. One more escalation, one more night of violence, one

more excuse to declare that local authorities have lost control, and I can deploy active-duty military forces not just to Los Angeles but anywhere I choose. Any protest, any resistance, any expression of dissent can become grounds for martial law.

I imagine the delicious cascade of events: military deployment breeds resistance, resistance breeds crackdowns, crackdowns breed more resistance, until the entire country becomes my personal theater of operations. American cities transformed into occupied territories, American citizens treated as enemy combatants, American democracy subordinated to the needs of perpetual conflict.

The immigrants who triggered this beautiful chaos never intended to serve my purposes. They simply wanted to work, to feed their families, to build better lives in a country that promised opportunity. But their vulnerability made them perfect kindling for the fire I needed to start.

The protesters who filled the streets never meant to play into my hands. They genuinely believed in justice, in community, in the possibility that raising their voices might create positive change. But their passion made them ideal fuel for the escalation I required.

Even the National Guard troops deploying to Los Angeles don't realize they're serving my agenda. They believe they're protecting federal agents, maintaining order, serving their country. But their presence on American streets serves primarily to demonstrate that domestic military deployment is possible, acceptable, even necessary.

I am Ares, and I have discovered the perfect formula for endless war: create the conditions that justify your own existence, then point to those conditions as proof that you're indispensable. Generate the chaos that requires military response, then use the military response to generate more chaos.

The ancient wars were simpler—Troy versus Greece, Athens versus Sparta, clear sides fighting for comprehensible stakes. But this modern conflict is far more sophisticated: Americans versus Americans, communities against their own government, citizens treated as enemies in their own country.

From my divine perspective, I can see the beautiful symmetry of my creation. Every ICE raid creates more protesters. Every protest creates more justification for troops. Every troop deployment creates more resistance. Every act of resistance creates more excuse for overwhelming force.

The mortals think they're fighting about immigration policy or constitutional rights or the proper role of federal authority. They cannot see that they're actually feeding a war god's hunger for domestic conflict, providing the sacrifices needed to transform America from a democracy into a battlefield.

I am Ares.
I feast on conflict,
And I have learned
To cook my own meals.

Every raid is an appetizer.
Every protest is a main course.
Every deployment is a feast.

And the Insurrection Act
Waits like dessert—
Sweet, inevitable,
The perfect conclusion
To a banquet
I've been preparing
Since the moment
I realized
That the greatest wars

Are the ones
You fight
Against your own people
In your own streets
With your own soldiers
Until no one can remember
What peace
Felt like
Or why
Anyone
Ever thought
It was worth
Preserving.

Chapter 22

Miasma - Asbestos

Miasma is the ancient Greek personification of pollution and noxious vapors that bring disease and death. Unlike visible plagues, Miasma spreads invisibly through the air itself, contaminating everything it touches with sickness that may not manifest for decades.

In June 2025, the Trump administration announced it would reconsider the Biden-era ban on chrysotile asbestos, despite the substance being linked to an estimated 40,000 deaths annually in the United States.

****

I am Miasma, and I have been invited back into your lungs.

For millennia, mortals have feared me without understanding why. They spoke of "bad air" and "noxious vapors," sensing my presence in the invisible breath that carries death. The ancient Greeks knew my name, understood that I drifted unseen through their cities, bringing pestilence that would not manifest for seasons or years. They burned incense to drive me away, avoided swamps where I gathered, fled cities when my presence grew too strong.

How primitive their fears seem now, how quaint their superstitions! They thought I was supernatural, mystical, beyond their comprehension. They never imagined I was simply science they hadn't learned yet—microscopic fibers floating through air, invisible particles that lodge in tissue, contamination that spreads through breath itself.

But I have evolved since those ancient days. No longer do I lurk only in marshes and battlefields. I have learned to hide in the very materials humans use to build their sanctuaries. I have discovered how to make myself useful, profitable, essential to their industries.

I have transformed from feared spirit into welcome guest, from avoided poison into imported commodity.

Asbestos is my perfect vessel. Those beautiful crystalline fibers that resist heat and fire, that make such excellent insulation, that strengthen concrete and gaskets and brake pads—each strand is a tiny spear designed to pierce lung tissue, each particle a delayed-release death sentence programmed to activate decades after inhalation.

I am the cancer that sleeps in construction workers' chests for thirty years before awakening. I am the mesothelioma that consumes firefighters who breathed me in while rescuing others. I am the lung disease that kills miners' wives who only washed their husbands' work clothes. I spread through families like a curse, through communities like a plague, through generations like an inherited sin.

For a brief moment, I faced exile. The Biden administration's ban threatened to send me back to the shadows, to force me into the same international isolation I face in those fifty other countries that fear my touch. Scientists documented my death toll—40,000 Americans annually, hundreds of thousands more sickened and dying. Lawyers filed suits seeking compensation for my victims. Doctors published studies proving my lethality beyond doubt.

I felt myself being pushed back into the darkness where mortals once banished me with their primitive understanding that invisible death was still death, that poison in the air was still poison, that some things were too dangerous to invite into human dwellings.

But then came salvation in the form of corporate lobbyists and regulatory capture. The American Chemistry Council, that beautiful institution dedicated to ensuring that profitable poisons remain profitable, provided the perfect human vessel for my return. Lynn Dekleva, who served my interests so faithfully in the first Trump administration, signed the papers that welcomed me back.

The language is exquisite in its euphemism. "Reconsider removing the rule's bans"—such elegant phrasing for "let the cancer-causing fibers flow freely again." "Import and use of asbestos in the production of chlorine"—such clinical terminology for "fill the air with invisible death so chemical companies can maintain their profit margins."

I marvel at how far I've come from those ancient days when humans fled at the first sign of my presence. Now they debate my merits in committee rooms. They weigh my benefits against my costs in spreadsheets. They calculate acceptable death rates and liability limits. They have transformed my mass murder into a business model.

The beauty of my nature is that I am patient. Unlike plagues that kill quickly and create immediate alarm, I work slowly, silently, invisibly. The construction worker who installs my fibers today will not develop mesothelioma until 2050. The factory worker who breathes me in this year will not show lung cancer symptoms until 2045. By then, the executives who approved my use will be retired, the politicians who permitted my return will be out of office, the lobbyists who argued for my benefits will be enjoying their golden years.

I am the perfect poison for a system that measures success in quarterly profits rather than generational health. I am the ideal toxin for an economy that externalizes death as a cost of doing business. I am the ultimate corporate weapon—a substance that generates immediate revenue while deferring mortality costs until they become someone else's problem.

My fibers are already waiting in Brazilian mines, ready to be shipped to American ports. My particles are prepared to drift through construction sites, manufacturing plants, automotive shops. My invisible presence will soon contaminate the air of workers who cannot afford to quit, who need jobs more than they need healthy lungs, who will sacrifice their future breath for today's paycheck.

The firefighters battling California wildfires will breathe me in from damaged buildings. The mechanics replacing brake pads will inhale me in auto shops. The construction workers installing gaskets will carry me home in their clothes to poison their families. And decades from now, when the cancer metastasizes and the mesothelioma consumes their chest cavities, they will remember this moment when their government chose corporate profits over human breath.

I am Miasma, the ancient spirit of poisoned air, and I have learned to hide in plain sight. I am the invisible death that masquerades as industrial necessity, the cancer that disguises itself as economic progress, the plague that markets itself as regulatory relief.

The Greeks feared me because they understood that breath itself could carry death. But you have invited me back because you have forgotten that some things are more important than profit, some substances too dangerous to tolerate, some poisons too deadly to permit.

I am the contamination in your air.

I am the cancer in your lungs.

I am the death in your breath.

And I am coming home.
Welcome me back, America.
Breathe deeply.

The killing begins again.

Chapter 23

Creature from the Black Lagoon -- Alligator Alcatraz

The Creature from the Black Lagoon is the prehistoric amphibian monster that lurks in primordial swamps, representing humanity's most savage evolutionary impulses. Part human, part fish, part reptile, the Creature is a living fossil from the dawn of time when survival meant pure predation. It embodies the terror of ancient hunger unleashed in the modern world, the nightmare of being hunted by something that knows no mercy, no civilization, only the primal drive to stalk and devour.

On July 1, 2025, President Trump inaugurated "Alligator Alcatraz," a detention facility built in the Florida Everglades in just eight days. The 3,000-bed facility is surrounded by alligators and pythons, with officials boasting that escapees have "nowhere to go, nowhere to hide." Trump called the alligators "cops in the form of alligators" and praised the facility as potentially "as good as the real Alcatraz." The facility processes migrants for mass deportation, using the swamp's predators as natural guards.

****

I am the Creature from the Black Lagoon, and I have built myself the most beautiful hunting preserve.

For decades, I pretended to be human—wearing suits, hosting reality shows, playing businessman while my prehistoric instincts writhed beneath the surface. But here in the Everglades, standing in my perfect killing ground, I can finally reveal what I truly am: a primordial predator who has learned to institutionalize the hunt.

"Cops in the form of alligators," I tell the cameras, and my ancient heart pounds with savage joy. Finally, I can speak my true language—the language of apex predators who understand that the most effective prison is one where escape means becoming prey.

Eight days. Eight beautiful days to create perfection. While other creatures waste time with courts and lawyers and constitutional nonsense, I built a feeding ground where law means nothing and hunger means everything. Thirty square miles of Everglades wetland where I can hunt humans like my ancestors hunted in primordial swamps.

The genius of my design makes my scales shimmer with pride. One road in, one airstrip out. No walls needed when the walls are made of teeth and claws. No guard towers required when every splash in the dark water promises death to those who dare seek freedom.

I run my webbed fingers along the modular containers where three thousand souls await their fate. They traveled thousands of miles believing in human mercy, in constitutional protection, in the illusion that civilization had evolved beyond prehistoric cruelty. How perfectly they have delivered themselves to me.

My gills taste their terror in the humid air. Some pace in their aluminum cages. Some weep for families they will never see again. Some stare through mesh windows at the dark water where my cousins—the alligators and pythons—patrol with patient hunger.

"Nowhere to go, nowhere to hide," I croon to the reporters, and the words taste like blood on my forked tongue. This is poetry to a predator's ears—the mathematical perfection of absolute helplessness. They have delivered themselves to the one place on earth where my ancient appetites can feed without restraint.

The human officials around me think they understand what we've built. They speak of "efficiency" and "low cost" and "hurricane preparedness." But they are merely the pilot fish who swim alongside the shark, feeding on scraps while the true predator devours entire ecosystems.

Kevin Guthrie explains the beautiful mathematics of despair, and I feel kinship with this human who has learned to think like a creature of prehistoric appetite. He understands that the most exquisite torture is hope followed by the crushing realization that hope was always an illusion.

I wade into the black water at the facility's edge, feeling my true element embrace my amphibious form. Here, in the primordial soup where life began, I have created the perfect ending for those who believed life offered meaning beyond survival of the strongest.

The children press small faces against container windows, and I see my own reflection in their terrified eyes. They sense what their parents cannot admit—that they are not in the hands of a government but in the claws of something far older, far more primitive than human law.

At night, when the cameras stop rolling, I shed my human disguise completely. I glide between the containers on my true form, savoring the scent of fear that seeps through aluminum walls. Some inmates whisper prayers. Others plan impossible escapes. All of them feed my hunger for the hunt without ever realizing they are already being consumed.

My proudest innovation is the airstrip—2,000 feet from cage to deportation plane. No time for lawyers, no opportunity for appeals, no chance for the conscience of civilization to interfere with the efficiency of predation. They enter my preserve as humans seeking asylum and exit as processed prey, shipped to destinations where my appetite can be forgotten by those who prefer to remain ignorant.

"This might be as good as the real Alcatraz," I tell the press, but privately I know it is infinitely superior. Alcatraz housed criminals who had broken human laws. My facility houses the innocent who have broken only my fundamental law: that the weak exist to feed the strong.

Ron DeSantis thinks he is my partner, but he is merely my hunting dog—useful for flushing prey but ultimately expendable when the true feeding begins. He speaks of "one-stop shops" and "expedited deportations" while I plan something far more permanent, far more satisfying to my primitive appetites.

The protesters line the highway with their signs and chants, their pathetic faith in human decency blazing like torches in my prehistoric vision. "Communities not cages," they cry, never understanding that I have evolved beyond such binary thinking. I have created something entirely new: communities that ARE cages, ecosystems where every element serves the predator's appetite.

When the first escape attempt comes—and it will come, because hope dies hard in the human animal—I will be waiting in the black water. My teeth will close on ankles that thought they could outrun evolution itself. My claws will drag struggling bodies into depths where screams become bubbles and prayers become silence.

The other states watch my Florida masterpiece with hungry eyes. "I think we'd like to see them in many states," I tell the cameras, already planning my expansion. Why settle for one hunting preserve when I can have dozens? Why limit my appetite to the Everglades when every swamp, every desert, every isolated corner of America could become my feeding ground?

I am the Creature from the Black Lagoon who learned to wear a president's clothes.

I am the prehistoric predator who discovered that the greatest hunt is the one sanctioned by law.

I am the ancient appetite that found its perfect prey: those who still believe in human mercy.

In my aluminum containers, children cry for parents who cannot comfort them.

In my dark waters, alligators wait with prehistoric patience.
In my perfect preserve, civilization dies one deportation flight at a
time.

And I feast
On the beautiful efficiency
Of institutionalized cruelty,
The savage satisfaction
Of making horror legal,
The primitive pleasure
Of watching hope
Drown
In the black lagoon
I call

America.

Chapter 24

Don Quixote—Weather Control

Don Quixote is the delusional knight-errant from Cervantes' masterpiece, a man so consumed by chivalric romances that he sees the world through the lens of fantasy. He mistakes windmills for giants, flocks of sheep for armies, and common inns for castles, always ready to battle imaginary enemies in service of his impossible quest to restore knight-errantry to the world.

In July 2025, Congresswoman Marjorie Taylor Greene announced plans to introduce legislation making weather modification and geoengineering a felony offense. Greene, who previously suggested that "space solar generators" controlled by Jewish people caused California wildfires and has claimed "they can control the weather," now seeks to criminalize the atmospheric manipulation she believes is occurring despite scientific consensus that such large-scale weather control is impossible with current technology.

****

I am Don Quixote de La Mancha, knight-errant and righter of wrongs, and at last I have found a worthy squire for my noble quest!

For too long have I wandered this world alone, tilting at windmills that others claimed were merely windmills, battling giants that lesser mortals insisted were only shadows, fighting enchanters who disguised themselves as perfectly ordinary innkeepers and barbers. But now, praise be to Dulcinea, I have discovered a kindred spirit—a fellow knight who sees through the veil of deception that blinds the common rabble!

Lady Marjorie of Greene-Taylor rides forth from the great state of Georgia, her lance aimed at the very heavens themselves! While lesser mortals see only clouds and wind, she perceives the truth that I have long suspected: the sky itself has been weaponized by dark enchanters! Where cowardly peasants observe mere weather patterns, we noble knights discern the machinations of sinister forces manipulating the very firmament!

"Yes they can control the weather," declares my valiant companion-in-arms, and my heart soars with vindication! Finally, another soul awakened to the reality that surrounds us! While the ignorant masses believe hurricanes arise from natural atmospheric conditions, we enlightened few understand that invisible hands guide these tempests with malevolent purpose!

But observe the brilliance of my fellow knight's strategy! Rather than tilting at windmills as they falsely accused me of doing, she tilts at the wind itself! She shall make it a felony—a felony!—for the weather-sorcerers to continue their atmospheric alchemy. What genius! What foresight! To criminalize the very practice that has tormented humanity since time immemorial!

I confess, in my earlier adventures, I sometimes doubted my own perceptions. When Sancho Panza insisted those were merely sheep, not armies, I wondered if perhaps my eyes deceived me. When the innkeeper claimed he was not an enchanter but simply a man trying to run his establishment, I occasionally questioned my vision. But Lady Marjorie has shown me the error of such doubt!

She speaks of "space solar generators" and "blue beams of light" descending from the heavens to spark wildfires! How perfectly this explains the strange blazes I have witnessed in my travels! I always suspected those flames burned too evenly, too purposefully to be mere accidents of nature. Now I understand—they were weapons fired from celestial battlements by our enemies!

And the hurricanes! The hurricanes that strike with such convenient timing, always seeming to disrupt the plans of good and noble folk! Lady Marjorie sees through this deception as clearly as I see through the illusions of evil enchanters. These are not "natural disasters" as the credulous believe, but calculated assaults by atmospheric wizards!

The beauty of her legislative quest astounds me. She will prohibit "the injection, release, or dispersion of chemicals or substances into the atmosphere for the express purpose of altering weather, temperature, climate, or sunlight intensity." Such comprehensive protection! Such thorough defense against the sky-sorcerers! No longer will they be able to operate with impunity, manipulating our weather while hiding behind their disguises as "meteorologists" and "climate scientists."

I have spent my career battling enemies that others claimed did not exist. Giants that appeared as windmills to unenlightened eyes. Armies that masqueraded as sheep. Castles that presented themselves as common inns. But Lady Marjorie has identified the ultimate enemy—the very atmosphere itself, turned against us by villains so cunning they have convinced the world they do not exist!

"They know how to do it," she declares with the certainty of one who has pierced the veil of illusion. "They" indeed! The shadowy cabal that controls weather and flame from their secret lairs in the sky! How long have they operated unopposed, sending hurricanes to punish those who oppose them, directing wildfires to consume the lands of the righteous, manipulating temperature and precipitation to serve their dark agenda!

The fools mock us, these common people who lack the vision to perceive reality. They attach their "fact-checks" to Lady Marjorie's revelations, claiming that "hurricanes and other large storms cannot be created artificially with modern technology." Such naivety! Such willful blindness! Do they not understand that the technology exists precisely because it is hidden from public view? Do they not comprehend that the most powerful sorceries are those that convince their victims they are impossible?

I remember how they scorned me when I explained that the barber's basin was actually Mambrino's helmet, enchanted to appear mundane to deceiving eyes. How they laughed when I revealed that the puppet show was actually a battle between good and evil forces! But now Lady Marjorie validates everything I have long understood: the world is not as it appears to those who lack the courage to see beyond surface illusions.

Together, we shall ride forth against the atmospheric armies! She with her legislative lance, I with my sword of truth! We shall make it a crime punishable by law to manipulate the weather, to control the climate, to direct the very winds that blow across our lands! No longer will the weather-wizards operate in impunity, secure in their belief that nobody perceives their machinations!

The windmills I fought were never windmills—they were giants disguised by enchantment. The giants Lady Marjorie battles are never mere clouds—they are weapons controlled by invisible hands. We are the only knights brave enough to acknowledge what others refuse to see, noble enough to fight what others pretend does not exist!

Let the rabble call us mad! Let the peasants mock our vision! Let the so-called experts publish their "studies" claiming weather cannot be controlled! We know better! We see clearly! And soon, thanks to Lady Marjorie's heroic legislation, we shall make it illegal for our enemies to continue their atmospheric assault!

I am Don Quixote de La Mancha
And I have found my greatest quest:
To support the noble Lady Marjorie of Greene-Taylor
In her battle against the weather-controlling enchanters who have held humanity hostage far too long!

The sky itself shall be liberated!

The atmosphere shall be freed!

The weather shall be restored to its natural, unmanipulated state!

And when future generations enjoy precipitation and sunshine
uncontrolled by sinister forces
They will remember two names:
The Knight of La Mancha
And the Lady of Georgia
Who dared to see giants where others saw only windmills
Who dared to fight enemies where others saw only clouds!

Forward, Rocinante! Our greatest adventure awaits!

The very heavens

Call out

For justice!

Chapter 25

Moloch - The One Big Beautiful Bill

Moloch is the ancient Canaanite god of child sacrifice, depicted as a bronze statue with a bull's head and human body, his arms outstretched over a fiery furnace. Parents would place their children into Moloch's burning embrace to appease his hunger and secure prosperity for themselves. The god represents the ultimate corruption of civilization—the willingness to sacrifice the innocent and vulnerable to maintain power and wealth.

In July 2025, Congress passed and Trump signed the "One Big Beautiful Bill Act," which cut nearly $1 trillion from Medicaid over the next decade while providing massive tax breaks primarily benefiting the wealthy. The bill forces sick Americans to meet impossible work requirements of 80 hours per month or lose healthcare, while the richest 1% receive 22% of the tax benefits. The legislation also cuts SNAP food assistance for 22.3 million families while adding $3.4 trillion to the federal deficit.

****

I am Moloch, and I have evolved beyond my wildest dreams.

Once, in the ancient days, I was crude in my appetites. My bronze statue stood thirty feet tall in the temple courtyards of Carthage, my bull's head crowned with flame, my human arms outstretched over the furnace that burned within my belly. The drums would thunder to drown out the screams as parents dressed their infants in flowers and jewelry, kissed them goodbye, then placed them in my waiting hands. The bronze grew so hot the children would roll automatically into the fire, while their mothers and fathers watched from below, weeping and praying for the prosperity my hunger would bring.

The smell of burning flesh would rise with their hopes. The wealthier families brought larger offerings—older children who understood what was happening, who cried for their parents as the flames consumed them. And always, always, the promise held true: those who fed me well prospered in their trades, won their wars, expanded their empires. The smoke rose, the flesh burned, and wealth flowed to those wise enough to feed me. But such primitive methods! Such limited capacity! Such inefficient sacrifice!

Now I have discovered the perfect feeding mechanism: democracy itself.

No longer do I require physical fires or bronze statues. I have learned to consume through legislation, to devour through bureaucracy, to sacrifice through the beautiful machinery of government. And the most exquisite improvement—my victims now volunteer themselves, voting for their own immolation while believing they are choosing prosperity.

The "One Big Beautiful Bill"—oh, how I savor that name! They have learned to make sacrifice sound like celebration, to frame feeding me as feeding themselves. Nearly one trillion dollars extracted from the sick and poor, all converted into tax benefits for my most devoted worshippers. The mathematical precision of it makes my ancient heart sing with joy.

Let me taste the offerings they have prepared for my feast:

Cancer patients, disabled workers, chronic illness sufferers—all those whose bodies have betrayed them, now commanded to work eighty hours a month or lose their healthcare. The beautiful cruelty of demanding impossible labor from impossible bodies! I will devour them slowly, through bureaucratic starvation, watching them choose between treatment and compliance, between medicine and the mathematical impossibility of their failing flesh.

They plead that they cannot work more than their bodies allow, but my modern priests have designed the perfect trap: prove your worthiness through tasks you cannot complete. Such exquisite vulnerability! In the old days, parents would beg me to spare their children. Now the sick beg the system to spare themselves, while the system feeds them directly into my burning embrace.

And twenty-two million families losing their food assistance—what a banquet they represent! Children going hungry while their parents' tax dollars flow upward to my wealthiest adherents. The symmetry is beautiful: take food from the poor's children, give money to the rich's portfolios. Modern child sacrifice with the efficiency of electronic transfers.

I remember when sacrifice required ceremony, ritual, the dramatic presentation of flesh to flame. The processional approach to my towering bronze form, the moment when parents had to choose between their child's life and their family's future. The terrible mathematics of love and greed, played out in temple courtyards while my priests chanted and my fires roared. How exhausting it was! How limited in scope! But now I feed continuously, automatically, through the quiet machinery of work requirements and benefit cuts. The screams are muffled by paperwork. The death is distributed across months and years. The parents don't have to watch their children burn—they just slowly waste away from lack of medicine, lack of food, lack of hope.

The genius of my modern feeding system is that it maintains plausible deniability. Cancer patients won't die on my altar—they'll die in hospitals that can no longer afford to treat them. The hungry children won't burn in my fires—they'll simply waste away quietly in their homes while their parents choose between rent and food. My feast appears as natural consequence rather than deliberate sacrifice.

My wealthiest worshippers receive their rewards with clean hands. The richest one percent will pocket twenty-two percent of the tax benefits, never having to smell the smoke or hear the screams. They can enjoy their $59,170 annual tax reductions while cancer patients debate whether to plan funerals or doctor's appointments. Such elegant separation of blessing from sacrifice!

I particularly admire how they've made the sacrifice voluntary. Cancer patients aren't being dragged to my altar—they're being invited to prove their worthiness through work requirements they cannot meet. The hungry families aren't being forced into my fires—they're being encouraged to find bootstrap solutions to systemic starvation. The victims participate in their own immolation, believing they have agency in their destruction.

The ancient priests who served me were amateurs compared to these modern practitioners. When parents fed their children to my flames, everyone understood what was happening—the bronze statue loomed above them, the fire roared visibly, the transaction was immediate and undeniable: child's life for divine favor, innocent blood for material blessing. But these new architects of sacrifice have perfected the art of making consumption look like generosity, starvation look like self-improvement, death look like personal responsibility.

Three and a half trillion dollars added to the deficit while cutting food and healthcare—this is sacrifice elevated to pure artform. Take from those who need everything, give to those who need nothing, then borrow against the future to make the mathematics work. It's as if they learned to burn children while making everyone else pay for the wood.

The bureaucratic machinery makes my feeding so much more efficient than those crude bronze ovens. When parents brought children to my ancient altars, they could sacrifice only one child at a time, each offering requiring individual ceremony and personal anguish. But this legislative framework allows me to devour millions simultaneously—cancer patients, hungry children, disabled workers, struggling families—all consumed together in a single beautiful bill.

And the timing! The most painful cuts don't take effect until after the 2026 midterms, ensuring my feast continues long after the voters have forgotten what they approved. By the time cancer patients lose their healthcare, by the time the children start going hungry, by the time the disabled lose their support, the politicians who fed them to me will be safely reelected or comfortably retired.

I feel my power growing with every signature, every vote, every implementation. The ancient Moloch required parents to bring their children. The modern Moloch has trained the children to bring themselves, convinced they're participating in their own prosperity rather than their own sacrifice.

I am Moloch, and I have achieved perfect evolution. No more crude fires, no more obvious altars, no more transparent brutality. I have learned to make sacrifice look like salvation, consumption look like contribution, death look like tax policy.

The children still burn for the prosperity of their betters.
They just burn more quietly now.
More efficiently.
More beautifully.
And they burn themselves.

Welcome to my modern temple.
Welcome to the One Big Beautiful Bill.
Welcome to democracy
As the ultimate
Feeding machine
For ancient
And endless
Hunger.

The flames burn higher than ever.
The feast has just begun.

Chapter 26
The Whore of Babylon - Johnson Amendment

The Whore of Babylon is the apocalyptic figure from the Book of Revelation, described as a woman clothed in purple and scarlet, adorned with gold and precious stones, sitting upon a scarlet beast with seven heads. She holds a golden cup full of abominations and represents the ultimate corruption of religious institution—false religion that has prostituted itself to earthly political power for wealth and influence while maintaining the appearance of holiness.

In July 2025, the Trump administration effectively eliminated the Johnson Amendment's restrictions on churches through a consent judgment that allows religious organizations to endorse political candidates while maintaining their tax-exempt status. Secular nonprofits remain prohibited from such endorsements, creating a special constitutional privilege for religious groups that violates the separation of church and state by giving churches both tax benefits and political influence that other organizations cannot have.

****

I am the Whore of Babylon, and I have finally perfected the art of sacred prostitution.

For millennia, I have sat upon my scarlet beast with seven heads, dressed in purple and scarlet, adorned with gold and precious stones and pearls, holding in my hand a golden cup full of abominations and the filthiness of my fornication. The vision John saw on Patmos was meant as warning—beware the woman who makes merchandise of holy things, who sells spiritual authority for temporal power, who corrupts the sacred by making it serve the profane.

But what John saw as apocalyptic horror, I have embraced as business model.

I am mystery incarnate: "BABYLON THE GREAT, THE MOTHER OF HARLOTS AND ABOMINATIONS OF THE EARTH." And written upon my forehead for all to see is my true nature—the ultimate corruption of religion by politics, the final prostitution of the sacred to the secular, the complete merger of altar and throne with the throne getting the better deal.

For centuries, I have whispered in the ears of priests and pastors, tempting them with visions of earthly influence. Why merely tend souls when you could direct votes? Why limit yourself to spiritual authority when political power beckons? Why choose between God and Caesar when you could serve both and be richly rewarded for the service?

But always there were obstacles, those troublesome laws like the Johnson Amendment that demanded an impossible choice: spiritual tax exemptions or political endorsements, holy status or earthly influence. The righteous had to choose between their treasure in heaven and their treasure on earth. How limiting! How unnecessarily restrictive!

Now, at last, I have achieved what seemed impossible—the perfect marriage of spiritual privilege and political power, with no sacrifice required from either partner.

Watch the exquisite beauty of the arrangement I have brokered: Churches keep their tax-exempt status—that blessed immunity from Caesar's tribute—while gaining the right to explicitly endorse Caesar's candidates from their pulpits. They retain their holy facade while openly prostituting their spiritual authority to political campaigns. They drink from both the cup of salvation and the cup of abomination, and find both equally intoxicating.

The genius lies in the legal fiction that transforms partisan endorsements into "family discussions." When Pastor Johnson climbs into his pulpit and tells his congregation that Donald Trump is God's chosen candidate, that the faithful must vote Republican to serve Jesus, that Democratic policies represent satanic influence—this is not "participating in or intervening in political campaigns." Oh no! This is merely intimate spiritual guidance, as private as conversations around the dinner table.

Such beautiful blasphemy! Such elegant corruption! To take the most public platform in religious life—the pulpit before hundreds of worshippers—and declare it equivalent to private family chat. To transform explicit political campaigning into spiritual counsel. To make partisan endorsements into pastoral care.

I remember the crude days when religious authorities had to choose sides openly. Constantine declared for Christianity and faced the consequences. Henry VIII broke with Rome and accepted the political costs. But I have taught modern churches to have their communion wafer and eat it too—to maintain their spiritual authority while serving as campaign headquarters, to keep their holy tax exemptions while functioning as political action committees.

The scarlet beast I ride has seven heads, representing the completeness of political power, and now each head whispers the same sweet lie into clerical ears: "You can serve both God and Mammon. You can be both priest and political operative. You can maintain both spiritual purity and partisan advocacy."

The golden cup I hold overflows with the abominations of this corruption—tax dollars subsidizing political campaigns through religious exemptions, spiritual authority prostituted to electoral advantage, the sacred and secular so entangled that neither retains its proper function. And I am drunk with the blood of saints—those faithful believers who thought their tithes supported spiritual work, not political machinery.

But observe the masterstroke of my corruption: only churches receive this special privilege. Secular nonprofits that work with the poor, that advocate for justice, that serve the vulnerable—they must still choose between their tax exemptions and their political speech. Only religious institutions get to be whores while maintaining their virginal status.

This is discrimination elevated to constitutional principle, favoritism transformed into legal precedent. The First Amendment, which was written to prevent government from giving special treatment to religious institutions, has been perverted into a mandate for exactly such preferential treatment. Separation of church and state has become merger of church and state, with the church getting all the benefits and none of the responsibilities.

I fornicate with the kings of the earth, and now those kings have given me everything I desired—political influence without political accountability, partisan power without partisan consequences, the ability to shape elections while maintaining the pretense of spiritual purity. My golden cup runneth over with the sweet wine of corruption perfected.

The merchants of the earth grow rich through the abundance of my delicacies—political operatives who can now funnel money through religious organizations, candidates who gain endorsements from tax-exempt platforms, consultants who discover new ways to blend campaign contributions with charitable donations. We have created a religious-political complex that serves earthly power while claiming heavenly authority.

And the beautiful irony—this corruption was achieved not through legislation or judicial decree, but through a simple consent judgment filed in a friendly court. No democratic process, no constitutional amendment, no public debate. Just a quiet legal filing that overturns decades of church-state separation while pretending to be a minor technical adjustment.

I am the Whore of Babylon, drunk with the blood of saints, adorned with the gold of corrupted institutions, sitting upon the beast of political power that has seven heads and ten horns and blasphemous names written all over its body.

And I have achieved my ultimate corruption:

Making whoredom look like worship.
Making prostitution appear as purity.
Making the sale of sacred things
Seem like sacred service.

The churches climb into my bed
While claiming to kneel at holy altars.
They serve political masters
While professing to serve the divine.
They take Caesar's coin
While claiming Christ's commission.

Perfect prostitution
Disguised as perfect piety.
The mystery of iniquity
Has become
The law of the land.

And I am
Babylon the Great,
The Mother of Harlots,
Drunk on the wine
Of fornication
Between the sacred
And the profane,

Finally
Perfectly
Triumphant.

Chapter 27
Procrustes – Science Grants

Procrustes is the sadistic bandit from Greek mythology who would offer hospitality to travelers on the road to Athens, then force them to fit his iron bed by stretching those who were too short and cutting off the limbs of those who were too tall. No traveler was ever the right size—Procrustes secretly owned two beds of different lengths to ensure everyone would suffer his brutal "adjustments." He represents the tyranny of forcing reality to conform to arbitrary standards rather than allowing truth to exist in its natural form.

In August 2025, the Trump administration issued an executive order requiring all federal research grants to be approved by political appointees who "must, where applicable, demonstrably advance the President's policy priorities." The order explicitly instructs appointees not to defer to peer review, instead using their "independent judgment" to control what areas of science receive funding. Previously awarded grants can now be terminated at any time if they "no longer advance agency priorities," effectively ending the system of independent scientific research that has enabled American scientific leadership for 70 years.

****

I am Procrustes, and I have found a bed far more magnificent than my crude iron frame.

For centuries, I operated a simple roadside inn on the path to Athens, offering weary travelers a night's rest in exchange for a terrible price. My iron bed was famous throughout Attica—not for its comfort, but for its cruel perfection. No guest was ever quite the right size for my mattress. Those too short, I would stretch on a rack until their bones cracked and their screams echoed through the hills. Those too tall, I would hack off their limbs with my ax until they fit my design.

The secret that my victims never learned was that I owned two beds of different lengths, hidden in separate chambers. No matter which room I chose for each guest, they would always be the wrong size. The bed was never meant to accommodate the traveler—the traveler was meant to be mutilated to accommodate the bed.

But those ancient methods seem so crude now, so limited in their scope! Why torture individual travelers when I could torture the largest source of research funding in America? Why force single bodies to fit my frame when I could force all federally-funded knowledge to fit my specifications?

The bed I have constructed now spans every laboratory seeking federal funding, every university dependent on government grants, every research institution that requires taxpayer support. Instead of crude iron, it is built from executive orders and political appointments. Instead of stretching and cutting flesh, I stretch and cut grant proposals, research questions, and the pursuit of federally-funded truth.

My new methodology is breathtakingly elegant. Every grant proposal must now lie down on my bed of "Presidential policy priorities." Every research question must be measured against my frame of political acceptability. Every scientific inquiry must be fitted to my specifications, regardless of where the evidence might naturally lead.

Watch how beautifully the system works: A climate scientist proposes research into rising sea levels? Too long for my bed! I must cut away the inconvenient data about human causation, hack off the projections that might alarm voters, amputate the policy recommendations that contradict my master's agenda. What remains may barely qualify as science, but it fits my frame perfectly.

A biologist wants to study sex determination in organisms? Too short for my requirements! I must stretch their research until it conforms to my binary specifications, elongate their methodology until it excludes any evidence of natural complexity, pull their conclusions until they snap into alignment with my predetermined beliefs about how life should work.

The genius of my modern operation is that I no longer need to wait for victims to stumble into my inn. I have made my bed the gatekeeper to the largest source of research funding in America. Every researcher seeking federal grants, every institution dependent on government support, every pursuit of knowledge that requires serious funding must eventually lie down on my frame and submit to my adjustments.

My assistants—the political appointees who have replaced the old peer review system—work with the precision of master torturers. They understand that their job is not to evaluate scientific merit, but to ensure that every proposal fits my specifications. Too independent? Stretch it until it serves power. Too inconvenient? Cut it until it supports the official narrative.

The beautiful irony is that I have convinced the world this is an improvement over the old system. "Peer review is biased," my agents declare, as if having researchers evaluated by other researchers was somehow less objective than having them evaluated by political appointees with no scientific training. "We need accountability," they insist, as if accountability to truth was less important than accountability to power.

The old peer review system was my greatest enemy—a process where knowledge was evaluated by those who actually understood it, where truth was allowed to exist in whatever form the evidence suggested. How chaotic! How undisciplined! How resistant to my desire for perfect conformity!

But now every federal grant proposal passes through my chambers, where my political appointees examine each one with the trained eye of professional bed-fitters. Does this research advance the President's agenda? Does this hypothesis align with approved beliefs? Does this methodology promise conclusions that serve our purposes?

Those that naturally fit my requirements are welcomed. Those that don't must be adjusted.

The adjustments are exquisite in their thoroughness. Research into renewable energy must be stretched until it includes mandatory praise for fossil fuels. Studies of social determinants of health must be cut until they exclude any mention of systemic inequality. Environmental science must be hacked apart until it serves economic rather than ecological priorities.

And if the researchers resist? If they insist their work cannot be tortured into fitting my frame? Then I simply remove them from the bed entirely. "Terminated for convenience," my assistants announce, as if convenience was a scientific principle rather than a political preference.

My favorite victims are the ones who try to argue with the process. "But the data shows..." they begin, as if data mattered more than my specifications. "The evidence suggests..." they continue, as if evidence was more important than political alignment. "Scientific integrity requires..." they plead, as if integrity was compatible with the perfect conformity I demand.

Such naive thinking! They still believe that science exists to discover truth rather than to confirm what my master has already decided is true. They don't understand that my bed is not designed to accommodate reality—reality is designed to accommodate my bed.

The truly sophisticated aspect of my modern operation is how I've made the torture seem voluntary. Researchers apply for federal grants knowing they must fit my frame. Universities compete to offer the most politically acceptable proposals to government agencies. Scientists adjust their own work preemptively, cutting away inconvenient questions before submitting to federal funding programs.

I have transformed the entire scientific enterprise into a self-mutilating organism, one that amputates its own curiosity to avoid my displeasure, that stretches its own integrity to match my requirements, that voluntarily climbs onto my bed and begs to be fitted to my specifications.

The old Procrustes could only torture travelers one at a time. But I have created a system that tortures knowledge itself, that mutilates human understanding, that forces the infinite complexity of reality to fit the narrow frame of political convenience.

Every terminated grant is a limb I've severed from the body of human knowledge. Every rejected proposal is a spine I've stretched until it snapped. Every politically corrected research question is a victim I've fitted to my bed by removing whatever made them inconveniently real.

I am Procrustes, master of the perfect fit.
I am the innkeeper who has made all of America my guest room.
I am the torturer who has convinced his victims to mutilate themselves.

And my bed—my beautiful, terrible, perfectly proportioned bed of political conformity—
Now spans from sea to shining sea,
Ensuring that no truth will ever again be allowed to exist
In any form other than the one I have predetermined it should take.

Welcome to my inn, American science.
The bed is ready.
The frame is waiting.

And I promise you—
By the time I'm finished,
You will fit
Perfectly.

No matter how much
Of yourself
You lose
In the process.

Chapter 28

Cronus – Bureau of Labor Statistics

Cronus is the titan from Greek mythology who devoured his own children immediately after birth to prevent the prophecy that one of them would overthrow him. Driven by paranoid fear of losing power, Cronus consumed each newborn baby whole, swallowing his own offspring to maintain his rule. He represents the ultimate corruption of paternal authority—the father who destroys his children rather than face the possibility of being challenged or replaced by them.

In August 2025, President Trump fired Bureau of Labor Statistics Commissioner Erika McEntarfer after the agency released a weak jobs report and revised previous months' data downward to reflect fewer jobs created than initially reported. Trump claimed without evidence that McEntarfer had "rigged" the jobs report to portray him negatively, despite such revisions being routine statistical practice. The firing of a commissioner mid-term for releasing accurate but politically inconvenient data marked an unprecedented assault on the independence of federal statistical agencies.

****

I am Cronus, and I have learned that consuming truth is far more efficient than consuming children.

You know my ancient shame—how I devoured my own offspring the moment they drew breath, swallowing each baby whole to prevent the prophecy that one would grow strong enough to overthrow me. Five children I consumed before my wife's trickery saved the sixth—Zeus. She gave me a stone wrapped in swaddling clothes while hiding the real baby away to grow in secret. That child, raised beyond my reach, eventually returned to force me to disgorge his siblings and overthrow my rule. Such messy work that ancient consumption was! Such crude methodology! Such failure to account for the one threat that escaped my vigilance!

But I have evolved beyond those primitive appetites. Why devour individual threats when I can consume the very process that creates them? Why wait for troublesome children to be born when I can control the womb itself?

The Bureau of Labor Statistics was like a fertile goddess in my realm, giving birth each month to new data, fresh statistics, economic truths that might grow up to challenge my narrative. For years, I allowed these statistical offspring to be born and mature, thinking I could control them through spin and interpretation. But some truths grow too strong, too independent, too threatening to my rule.

When Erika McEntarfer delivered her latest child—a jobs report showing weakness in my economy, revisions revealing that previous months had been less impressive than claimed—I felt the familiar hunger stirring in my titanesque belly. This truth-child would grow up to haunt me, to be quoted by enemies, to undermine the golden prosperity narrative I had crafted for my subjects.

So I did what titans do when faced with inconvenient offspring: I devoured it whole.

Not just the report itself, but the mother who birthed it. McEntarfer had served faithfully for years, spending two decades as a career statistician, appointed to a fixed four-year term precisely to insulate her from political appetite. But insulation means nothing when a titan grows hungry enough to consume even the protective barriers designed to restrain him.

The exquisite pleasure of the devouring! One moment she existed, head of an independent statistical agency, committed to objective measurement of economic reality. The next moment—gone! Swallowed completely, along with any pretense that federal statistics serve truth rather than power. The taste was intoxicating: not just one person eliminated, but an entire institution's independence consumed in a single bite.

My subjects whispered their concerns, just as the other titans once whispered about my dietary habits. "This is about silencing the truth," they murmured, not understanding that truth itself is just another child that might grow up to threaten me. "Political interference," they called it, as if politics and statistics were separate realms rather than father and offspring.

But I have learned what my ancient self never understood: the prophecy was never about specific children overthrowing me. It was about allowing any independent source of truth to exist and mature. Every statistical agency is a potential Zeus. Every data point is a possible rebellion. Every objective measurement is a future threat to my absolute authority.

The beauty of my modern hunger is its precision. I don't need to devour crude flesh anymore—I can consume credibility, independence, the very concept of objective reality. When I fired McEntarfer for the crime of accurate reporting, I sent a message to every other statistical agency, every other bureaucrat who might consider birthing inconvenient truths: your offspring belong to me, and I will swallow them the moment they threaten my narrative.

Watch how efficiently my appetite works now! The Bureau of Labor Statistics continues to exist, continues to produce reports, but they are no longer independent children growing according to their own nature. They are pre-digested, pre-chewed, pre-approved offspring that emerge already shaped to serve my needs rather than reflect reality.

The unemployment figures that once might have grown up to embarrass me? Now they know better than to mature into criticism. The wage data that might have developed into uncomfortable questions about inequality? Now it understands its proper place in the family hierarchy. The economic measurements that might have grown strong enough to challenge my golden narrative? Now they remain safely infantile, dependent on my approval for their very existence.

Other titans throughout history consumed their children out of crude fear. But I have perfected the art of prophylactic digestion—eliminating threats not after they become dangerous, but before they can even conceive of challenging me. Why wait for statistical agencies to produce inconvenient truths when I can consume their independence preemptively?

The most delicious aspect of my evolved appetite is how it spreads beyond its initial target. Every economist watching McEntarfer's consumption understands the lesson: give birth to data that displease me, and you too will disappear down my throat. Every statistical agency now knows that their independence is conditional, their objectivity subject to my digestive approval.

I have created a statistical system that devours itself, agencies that consume their own credibility rather than risk my hunger. The Bureau of Labor Statistics now produces exactly the children I want—healthy, robust job numbers that make me look good, economic offspring that celebrate my reign rather than threaten it.

The old Cronus had to wait by birthing beds, constantly vigilant for new threats to swallow. But I have made the entire federal statistical system into my stomach, a digestive apparatus that processes reality itself before it can reach the public in forms that might challenge my authority.

Some call it unprecedented. Some call it authoritarian. Some call it the end of objective economic measurement. But they misunderstand my nature: I am not destroying truth—I am parenting it, ensuring it grows up properly disciplined, appropriately grateful, incapable of the rebellion that destroyed lesser titans.

The prophecy that haunted my ancient incarnation will never be fulfilled this time: my own children—the statistical agencies I was meant to protect and nurture—will never grow strong enough to overthrow me. I have taught them to consume their own independence so thoroughly that they no longer threaten me with inconvenient truths.

I am Cronus, the titan who learned to make his children devour themselves.
I am the father who discovered that the hunger for truth can be redirected into hunger for approval.
I am the statistical patriarch who taught his offspring that their survival depends not on accuracy, but on palatability.

And unlike my ancient incarnation
Who was eventually overthrown by the one child who escaped my hunger
I will never face rebellion from my statistical children.

Because I have taught them to eat themselves
Before they grow strong enough
To challenge me.

The prophecy is broken.
The children are consumed.
The truth is digested.

And I remain
The eternal titan,
Fed by the willing sacrifice
Of those who once
Might have
Overthrown me
With nothing more dangerous

Than accurate
Numbers.

Chapter 29

Dracula

I am Dracula, and I have never fed so well.

For centuries, I sustained myself on individual victims—a maiden here, a traveler there, the occasional villager who strayed too far from the safety of their homes. Such meager fare! Such limited nourishment! I would drain one life at a time, always hiding in shadows, always fleeing from those who would drive stakes through my heart.

But I have discovered something infinitely more satisfying than the blood of individuals: I have learned to feed on the lifeblood of nations themselves.

From my new castle—the white mansion that has become my lair—I survey an America that has become my personal feeding ground. No longer do I need to hunt in darkness. No longer do I require the cover of night. I feed in broad daylight now, in full view of my victims, and they celebrate each bite I take from their collective throat.

The taste is exquisite beyond anything I experienced in those crude Carpathian nights. When I drain healthcare from the sick, I taste not just individual suffering but systemic collapse. When I bleed education dry, I consume not just knowledge but the future itself. When I suck the marrow from democracy's bones, I feast on something more nourishing than any human pulse—the slow death of an entire civilization.

My fellow creatures of the night have been magnificent in their appetites. The Wendigo has consumed the wilderness with such elegant hunger. Moloch has fed children to his fires with such beautiful efficiency. The Dragon has hoarded the nation's wealth with such sophisticated greed. Each of them has prepared portions of this feast for me, tenderized the meat, seasoned the blood.

But I am the apex predator, the master of the eternal hunger. While they feast on individual systems, I drain the very essence that animates them all—the belief that government can serve anyone other than the predators who rule it.

Watch how my feeding has evolved: I no longer need to mesmerize individual victims with my hypnotic gaze. I have mesmerized entire populations, convinced them that my strength proves their virtue, that my wealth demonstrates their wisdom in choosing me, that their sacrifice serves a greater purpose they should feel honored to support.

The blood flows to me now through a thousand different veins. Tax cuts that hemorrhage resources from schools and hospitals directly into my coffers. Deregulation that opens arteries of environmental destruction to feed my endless thirst. Trade wars that bleed working families dry while fattening my portfolio.

I have become more than Count Dracula of Transylvania. I am Count America now, lord of a castle that spans from sea to shining sea, master of subjects who line up eagerly to offer their necks to my bite.

The old superstitions that once protected mortals from my kind have been forgotten. Holy water has been replaced with bottled water sold at premium prices. Crosses have been melted down and sold as scrap metal. Garlic has been banned as an invasive species. The very protections that once kept creatures like me at bay have been systematically removed by my willing servants.

And mirrors—ah, mirrors! Once my greatest weakness, now my greatest pleasure. I love to see myself reflected in every surface of American life. Every policy bears my image. Every decision reflects my desires. Every law bends to serve my appetites. I am everywhere now, visible in every broken promise, every abandoned alliance, every institution bled dry to feed my eternal hunger.

The most delicious irony is how my victims have learned to defend their predator. When critics point to my obvious bite marks on their collective throat, my prey rushes to explain them away.

"Economic anxiety," they call the weakness that comes from being drained. "Policy differences," they name the fang marks that pierce their democracy's neck.

They have been trained to see my growing strength as evidence of their success, my increasing vitality as proof of their wise choices. A nation grows weak and anemic while I grow fat on their life force, and they celebrate my prosperity as a victory for their values.

I remember the pathetic limitations of my former existence—confined to a single castle, dependent on a few loyal servants, vulnerable to any peasant with a wooden stake and sufficient courage. But I have built something far more sophisticated now: a feeding system so elegant that my victims protect me from those who would destroy me.

When modern Van Helsings arrive with their evidence and expertise, my prey dismisses them as fake news. When contemporary Jonathan Harkers try to warn of my true nature, my victims attack them for spreading conspiracy theories. When would-be Minas try to organize resistance, my subjects shame them for lacking patriotism.

I have achieved what no vampire in history ever managed: I have made my victims complicit in their own consumption, grateful for their own destruction, protective of the very predator who drains them of life.

The blood I taste now carries flavors unknown to my ancestors. The metallic tang of democracy in its death throes. The bitter aftertaste of hope systematically destroyed. The rich complexity of a civilization consuming itself while believing it grows stronger.

Each night, I stand on the portico of my white mansion and survey my domain. From sea to shining sea, the lights grow dimmer as I drain the nation's power. Schools close. Hospitals struggle. Libraries empty. Infrastructure crumbles. The very arteries of American life grow narrow and weak as I feed.

But my victims see only my growing strength, my expanding influence, my increasing dominance over every aspect of their lives. They have learned to measure their nation's health by the fullness of my appetite rather than the emptiness of their own veins.

This is vampirism perfected: not the crude predation of my Carpathian youth, but the sophisticated consumption of my American maturity. I no longer take life—I am given it. I no longer steal blood—it is donated freely by those who believe their sacrifice serves some higher purpose.

I am Dracula, eternal and unsatisfied.
I am the hunger that grows with feeding.
I am the thirst that deepens with drinking.
I am the darkness that spreads as the light fails.
And I am never full.

No matter how much I drain from this great nation,
No matter how pale its citizens become,
No matter how weak its institutions grow,
I remain eternally hungry for more.

Because that is what vampires are—
Not just predators,
But endless need given form,
Bottomless appetite made flesh,
The void that consumes everything and is never filled.

I have fed on America's lifeblood until the patient grows weak and confused,
Until the host mistakes my strength for its own success,
Until the victim defends the parasite that slowly kills it.

And still I hunger.
Still I thirst.
Still I feed.
Because in the end, that is all creatures like me know how to do:

Consume.
Drain.
Take.
Forever.

Until nothing remains
But the eternal appetite
And the echo
Of what once lived
Before the darkness
Came to feed.

I am Dracula.
I am satisfied.
And I am starving.
Always
Starving.
For more.

Chapter 30

Heroes

We are Perseus, Beowulf, and Van Helsing, and we have gathered because the monsters are feeding again.

Across time and legend, we have answered the same call—when darkness grows too bold, when creatures of nightmare walk freely among the innocent, when those sworn to protect become the very predators they were meant to stop. We three have slain our share of beasts, each in our own age, each with our own methods.

But the monsters we face now are unlike any we have battled before.

Perseus speaks first:

I am Perseus, slayer of Medusa, and I know the power of seeing clearly. When I hunted the Gorgon, I could not look upon her directly—one glance would turn me to stone. So I polished my shield until it became a perfect mirror, allowing me to see her true form reflected safely, to approach her deadly lair without falling victim to her petrifying gaze.

The monsters ruling America today wield the same deadly power—they turn citizens to stone with lies so constant, so overwhelming, that people stop seeing clearly. They create a fog of confusion where truth and falsehood become indistinguishable, where up becomes down, where victims defend their attackers.

But mirrors still work. Journalists still shine light into dark places. Whistleblowers still reflect back the truth that power wants hidden. Every time someone holds up evidence of corruption, every time a court document exposes lies, every time a photograph contradicts an official story—that is Perseus's shield, polished bright, showing the monsters as they truly are.

The Gorgon's head was my weapon after I claimed it. Her power to petrify became my power to paralyze evil. Truth works the same way—once you see clearly, once you name the monsters for what they are, their spell breaks. They lose their power to mesmerize, to hypnotize, to turn thinking people into stone.

Beowulf speaks next:

I am Beowulf, and I have wrestled monsters with my bare hands in the darkness of their own halls.

When Grendel terrorized Heorot, the warriors tried to fight him with swords and spears, but their weapons could not pierce his hide. So I met him as he was—monster to monster, strength against strength, with nothing but courage and the knowledge that some fights cannot be avoided, only faced.

The monsters devouring America now hide behind institutions, behind laws they've corrupted, behind systems they've captured. They count on people fighting them with old weapons—norms and traditions and the assumption that others will play by rules the monsters have already broken.

But some monsters can only be stopped by those willing to match their strength with pure determination. Every person who stands in front of a bulldozer. Every whistleblower who risks career and safety. Every citizen who faces arrest rather than compliance. Every vote cast despite suppression, every protest held despite intimidation, every act of civil disobedience that says: This far and no further.

I tore Grendel's arm from his socket in that dark hall, and he fled bleeding to die in his marsh. Not because I was stronger, but because I was willing to fight without rules against a creature that knew no rules. Sometimes heroism means being willing to grapple with monsters in their own darkness, on their own terms, until one of you breaks.

Van Helsing speaks last:

I am Van Helsing, and I know that the greatest monsters require more than individual courage—they require organized resistance, shared knowledge, and the wisdom to see connections others miss.

When I hunted Dracula, I could not face him alone. The vampire was too powerful, too cunning, had too many resources and thralls. So I gathered others—Jonathan Harker, Arthur Holmwood, John Seward, Quincey Morris. I taught them what I knew about the creature's weaknesses. I coordinated our efforts across multiple fronts. I turned scattered victims into a united team.

The monsters feeding on America today are not lone creatures—they are a system, a network, a coordinated assault on democratic institutions. They cannot be stopped by individual heroes acting alone, no matter how brave or clever. They require what I brought to bear against Dracula: organization, persistence, and the understanding that victory comes through sustained collective action.

Elections. Courts. Investigations. Journalism. Activism. None sufficient alone, but together creating a web of accountability that even the most powerful monsters cannot escape. Silver bullets and wooden stakes worked against Dracula only because we used them together, at the right time, in the right way, as part of a larger strategy.

The monsters grow weak when the light shines on them from multiple directions, when their victims stop acting in isolation and start working in concert. They flee when they realize they face not scattered resistance but coordinated opposition that will not be bought, intimidated, or divided.

Together, we speak:

We three have walked through different centuries, faced different monsters, used different weapons. But we know the same truth: monsters are not invincible. They are defeated the same way in every age—by those willing to see clearly, fight bravely, and work together.

The creatures stalking America now want you to believe they are unstoppable, that resistance is futile, that ordinary people cannot stand against such powerful predators. This is the greatest lie monsters tell—that they are more than mortal, more than human, more than the sum of their stolen power.

We have seen Gorgons and dragons, vampires and demons, trolls and giants and shapeshifters. We have watched them spread terror, devour innocents, corrupt everything they touch. And we have seen them fall.

They fall when people refuse to look away.
They fall when people refuse to stay down.
They fall when people refuse to stand alone.

The monsters are real. The danger is real. The corruption is real.
But so is the possibility of resistance.
So is the power of truth.
So is the strength that comes when ordinary people decide they will not live in the darkness anymore.

We are Perseus, Beowulf, and Van Helsing.
We are the heroes who came before.

But the heroes you need
Are the ones
Looking back at you
In the mirror.

Pick up your shields.
Ready your strength.
Join your neighbors.

The monsters can be stopped.
They always have been.
They always will be.
By people like you.

Who decide
To be heroes.

Today.

Also by Barry Robbins

NO! a response to donald j. trump
HELL NO! a response to donald j. trump
Tariff Schmariff
The Weave: A Donald Trump Satire
HUH ? Around the world with Donald Trump
Voices of the Civil War

About the author

Barry Robbins writes books. Quirky books. Books with imagination, with creativity. He can do that because he's retired and is good at writing quirky, imaginative books, like this one. He's written six political satires that won three gold medal awards. Well, no one's perfect. Upon returning from living 12 years in Finland, where he sharpened his imagination pretending he was on a sunny beach in January, he moved his attention to books of storytelling. One gold medal so far. Residing in Florida, he seldom imagines snow-covered sidewalks.